THE
PHYSICIAN

EVELYN ASTRA

OTHER BOOKS BY EVELYN ASTRA:

Table of Contents

Content Advisory:

This book contains strong sex scenes, direct depictions of cancer patients (including a parent who survived cancer and a cancer patient who dies), and direct depictions of a cheating ex.

For everyone who was told by someone they loved that
their dream was not realistic, or was 'too much'.
You really can have it all. Go get that bread, bitch.

PROLOGUE

Sophia clung to Eliot's arm as they strolled through the mall, each carefully measured step full of smugness and ecstasy. They were both dressed casually, but Soph knew that even in jeans and a plain white t-shirt, Eliot made heads turn — girls and guys alike. After dating for over three years, she was used to it. But that didn't stop the wonder and yes, smugness, that came with knowing that he had chosen her.

Today was making her *extra* smug, because it signalled the start of Eliot choosing her forever. As in for life. Because they were ring shopping.

Soph's smile grew even wider. Sure, she had seen this coming a mile away, but it felt incredible to finally be here. She imagined it wouldn't feel as good as him actually popping the question, but trying on rings with the love of her life and seeing the awe and love in his eyes as he looked at her?

Yeah, she could get used to this for the rest of her life.

The pair came to a stop in front of yet another jewellery store, communicating silently in the way only long-term partners could. Sophia relished the smile Eliot gave her as he pulled her through the doors, already beelining for the counter of sparkling diamonds.

Brushing a hand down his back, Soph analysed the rings silently, looking for one that would catch her eye. She loved bling as much as the next girl, but this ring was special. She wanted it to really stand out. After all, she'd only have the one — Eliot was her first boyfriend, but he would be her last.

From the moment they had met, they had clicked. After being friends for almost a decade through school, something finally shifted and they started dating as they started college. He was her best friend, her rock, the love of her life.

"Which ones do you like, my dear?" Eliot leaned down to murmur in her ear. Six foot whatever to her five foot three, he towered over her and the glass case.

Soph hummed indecisively. "I still can't choose, love. You might have to end up picking for me."

"You said that last time!" His low laugh in her ear made a shiver run down her spine.

God, the man was gorgeous — tall, six pack, floppy sandy hair that completed his surfer look and a face that was pretty but still heavily masculine. She wanted to lick every inch of him.

"You know what? I mean it this time. I know I want it to be special, but you know me best, and any ring from you is going to be special. I want you to pick it."

"You sure, babe? I want it to be perfect. You deserve absolutely perfect." Eliot's eyes probed hers, looking for reassurance.

He didn't have to look far. Soph would hand him the moon on a stick if he asked. And she knew he'd do the same for her.

"I'm sure, love. Having your ring on my finger, having the rest of my life with you? It's a privilege beyond measure. I love you so much."

Eliot pulled her gently towards him, wrapping his arms around her waist.

"I love you, Soph. You make me the happiest — and luckiest — man on Earth. I can't wait to make you my wife."

Sophia melted into his kiss, pulling away only when a polite cough sounded to her left.

"Oh! Sorry," she said sheepishly to the saleswoman.

"Don't worry about it, hun. We see it every day," the woman said with a wink. "Are there any rings here you'd like to try on?"

"As a matter of fact, yes," Eliot's deep voice cut in smoothly. "This one, please."

He pointed at a glimmering diamond ring in the corner, cushion cut with a high setting, sitting on a gold band studded with baguette diamonds. It was gorgeous. Not quite what Sophia would have chosen herself, not quite practical to wear under gloves while conducting research, but it was perfect because Eliot had picked it for her. She could always wear it around her neck while at work.

The saleswoman took it out and slipped it onto Sophia's ring finger, where it threw the light onto the surrounding surfaces as she turned her hand one way then the other.

"Wow," she whispered. She could feel the weight of it, but it still felt surreal seeing it on her.

"Wow," Eliot agreed, pressing a kiss to her temple. "It suits you so well. How much is it?"

The saleswoman gushed some more, talking to Eliot about clarity and cut and colour. Sophia wasn't listening, though. She just kept staring at her hand, imagining the moment Eliot would pull this out while on one knee. It would be perfect, she was sure. Eliot was perfect, and she would never stop being grateful for finding this generous, caring, funny, smart man, who treated her like a princess.

Soon, she thought to herself, as Eliot kept talking to the woman. Soon, this ring would be hers permanently, and they would be fiancés.

She couldn't wait.

CHAPTER 1

Two years later

Soph glared at her empty ring finger on the bus ride home from work. Traffic was insane tonight, but she had been impatient this whole week.

Two years ago, Eliot had found the ring of their dreams — but it had been far too expensive at the time. A few months ago, he had gotten a promotion at work, and had started acting slightly suspiciously: a little more secretive than usual, a bit jumpy, and she had even noticed advertisements on his Instagram feed for engagement planners.

This, combined with the fact that they were now in an advantageous financial situation, she was sure he was finally going to propose.

This weekend, to be precise, at their dinner date that he had planned and put in her calendar weeks ago.

Sophia turned her glare to the surrounding traffic, which had barely budged in the last half hour. She still had plenty of time to get ready for tonight, but she was supposed to meet Nef, her best friend, at her place to help choose an outfit. They would have planned this sooner, but Nef had been especially busy lately planning a new exhibition for the museum she co-owned with her fiancé, Xander.

Forty minutes later, Sophia finally arrived at her friend's place — a cozy but large townhouse in San Diego. Letting herself in with the spare key she'd been gifted, she headed straight up the staircase to her right and into the master bedroom.

"Oh good, you're here!" Nef was standing at the open walk-in closet, holding two dresses by the hanger in each hand. "I went ahead and started choosing options, I've laid most of them out on the bed."

Indeed, the bed, a normally neatly made king size monstrosity of blankets and colourful pillows, was covered in an array of pants, blouses, dresses, and even Sophia's old formal dress. The two friends had lugged some of Soph's clothes over weeks ago to prepare, but it had mostly sat in cardboard boxes until now.

Nef was still talking at the speed of light, her dark curls starting to fall around her face from where she had swept it up in a high bun. Sophia had always envied her curls, but knew that Nef had once envied her own wavy blonde hair. She supposed everyone always wanted what they didn't have, so had come to love her own locks as they were.

"— you got your nails done right??" Nef finished breathlessly as she pulled out yet another outfit.

"Who do you think I am? I've had my nails done for the last two years, babe." Soph flashed her French manicure.

Giving each other matching grins, Soph went to work trying on various clothes while Nef moved to the door next to the closet to start prepping the shower for her.

"What do you think of this one hun?" Soph called over the sound of the shower. The dress had been a tight squeeze, but standing in front of the mirror, Sophia loved the way it hugged her hips before falling to mid-calf, the cowl neck low enough to dip between her small breasts.

Popping her head out from the bathroom, Nef gave a quick once over, eyes widening.

"Oh. My. GOD! If I wasn't engaged myself, I'd ask you the question right now. That one is perfect. You have to wear it."

Sophia laughed, her eyes going straight to Nef's left hand — and the whopping emerald cut diamond that glittered on a gold band with more, smaller diamonds on it. It had been a month since her engagement, and she couldn't be happier for her best friend. Nef had gone through a lot, and she and Xander were perfect for each other.

Slipping out of the silvery material, Soph quickly dragged out her matching silver heels with the sparkly straps, and a small black handbag for her phone and lipstick. Putting them in a neat pile on the last clear spot on the bed, she kicked Nef out of the bathroom for her 'everything shower'.

An hour later, the bedroom was clean again, the closet full, and Sophia stood in front of Nef at the mirror as the taller brunette carefully curled Soph's hair with the flatiron.

Her mind slowly drifted in the comfortable silence. Five years with Eliot, and tonight was finally the night. It felt so surreal that her excitement felt almost dampened, as though she had been expecting this for so long it had almost lost that sense of surprise she had harboured when he had first asked her if she wanted to go ring shopping.

But it was real, she reminded herself. She was about to get engaged!

Years of dreaming of a life with Eliot were hours away from becoming reality. Not to say that just being partners wasn't enough of a life together already, but Sophia had always known she was a possessive person. She wanted everyone to see that she was taken, that they were committed for life officially and not just through whispered promises between kisses over the years.

"Done," Nef's low reverent whisper sounded loud in the silence of the bedroom. "Eliot is a very lucky guy."

Her smile was so wide it hurt her cheeks. "He knows it, too."

"He better," Nef replied. "It's almost six, Xander should be home soon and we can drive you to the restaurant?"

"Thank you so much again, Nef. For all of this."

Nef waved a hand in dismissal. "Love, we established years ago we're ride or die. If I had missed this, I would have killed you. And I will still kill you if you don't send me photos immediately of the ring!"

Sophia laughed again, the sound drowned out by the opening and closing of the front door. A deep male voice filled the house, calling Nef's name.

Her friend flushed with pleasure, giving Soph a quick squeeze on the shoulder before hurrying out of the room to greet her fiancé. Soph drifted slowly to the stairs, waiting for the sounds of their PDA greeting to die down before showing her face.

"Hey, Xander. Long day at work?" The man in question was undoing his tie by the door, dark auburn hair ruffled and slightly dark circles under his ridiculously blue eyes. He and Nef were an abhorrently good looking couple.

"Hey, Sophia! Yeah, long day, had to put out a few fires for some potential sponsors. What about you though? You look great. Eliot is a very lucky man." Soph grinned at the way he echoed Nef's earlier statement.

"Excited, as you can imagine," she winked.

Xander chuckled, pressing a kiss to Nef's cheek as he moved through the hall towards the open plan living room and kitchen.

"I'm sure," he said. "Although I sympathise with Eliot. The man is absolutely a pile of nerves right now."

"Honey, you still good if we drop Soph off at the restaurant?" Nef cut in as they followed Xander through the house.

"Of course. Can't let you girls miss your last moments of friendship before you're both engaged women."

Soph looked away as they occupied themselves in yet another quick session of PDA. She was no prude, but she preferred to keep her physical romance private and out of sight — especially with the way her tastes ran.

A few minutes later, she sat in the back of Xander's Mercedes-Benz (he really was one rich bitch), makeup perfected and her stomach a pit of butterflies. Nef and Xander chatted quietly in the front, leaving her to her own thoughts.

Before she knew it, they had arrived.

It was a beautiful venue. 'Mr A's' was a French-American restaurant boasting stunning views of the San Diego skyline, known for its ambience and popularity for being a proposal destination. Decked with navy blue accents and clean wood and gold furniture, the place screamed luxury, intimacy, and romance.

In short, Eliot had chosen the perfect place. As usual.

"Thanks guys," Soph's voice was soft but strong. "Wish me luck!"

"You don't need it!" Nef cried as Xander wished her luck.

Grinning, she stepped out of the car and onto the street. Checking her phone again, she confirmed that Eliot was already inside at their table. She loved how he was always slightly early to things.

God, she was ready to say yes to this man.

Taking a deep breath, Soph savoured the feeling of being just a girlfriend, before she stepped into the building.

CHAPTER 2

Tingles ran down Soph's spine as she reached the rooftop bar.

The 360 degree windows were all thrown open, and a cool night breeze drifted in towards the central round bar. Navy stools and low chairs dotted the space, along with various tables covered in white tablecloths. The wooden ceiling had a variety of well-placed chandeliers dripping crystals, and the effect had heads turning as the light reflected off her dress like raindrops.

Only one turned head mattered though.

Eliot was dressed immaculately in a deep grey suit, his white shirt slightly open at the top. He sat at an intimate table set for two by the far window, his sandy hair artfully messy, his cheekbones sharp enough to cut in the light. And he was smiling sheepishly at her as she confidently moved towards him.

Sophia may or may not have added a bit of extra sway to her hips, just for fun.

Eliot stood up gracefully and kissed her cheek softly, a hand caressing her waist. It was the most PDA Soph could handle, and she was always grateful that he kept it to a minimum for her.

"You look… beyond gorgeous," Eliot's mouth was slightly open, his pupils wide as he took her in. He shook his head slightly and guided her to her seat, pulling the chair out for her.

"I mean it, Soph. You're divine."

She felt a blush unfurl over her cheeks, but she knew it was true. She had dressed like this for a reason.

"Thanks, love. You look amazing too," she said truthfully.

"I ordered your favourite wine," Eliot reached across the table as he sat back down, taking her hand in his. "I'm so glad you're here. How was work?"

He started lightly stroking his thumb over the back of her hand, and Soph could barely focus on recounting how Maurice, one of her lab mice, had bitten her coworker Jake while he was trying to collect a retro-orbital blood sample.

A waiter came over with a bottle of red, and Soph raised an eyebrow as Eliot quickly drained his glass, before pouring himself another. They had both been pretty big party-goers in college, but since they started working professionally — her as a medical researcher and Eliot as a marketing manager — they hadn't drunk much at all.

This was definitely a sign of nerves, which was really sweet. Didn't he realise that her answer was the most obvious yes?

Soph sipped carefully at her glass (in case there was a ring hidden at the bottom) as the pair traded stories about their day and updated each other about various friends and colleagues. They eventually ordered, and by the time they reached dessert, Sophia was ready to be rolled out of the restaurant.

She was also ready to ask the damn question herself if Eliot didn't make a damn move already.

Still, she forced herself to be patient as they shared a large slice of tiramisu, her favourite dessert. Halfway through, Eliot broke the contented silence as they ate.

"Hey darling, I wanted to talk about something with you."

Fucking finally.

Sophia sat up straighter, uncrossing her ankles and recrossing them under the table.

"Of course love. You know you can ask me anything." She smiled at him and reached forward to take his hand reassuringly.

Eliot smiled back weakly, before removing his hand and reaching for his pocket.

This was it. This was finally, finally, her dream coming true. This man she had loved for years, who she had grown with and supported and been loved by was about to become her fiancé.

Butterflies erupted in her stomach, her chest, and blood rushed in her ears. Time slowed down as Eliot slowly, so slowly, withdrew his hand from his pocket.

And blew his nose with a crumpled tissue.

"Darling, we need to break up."

CHAPTER 3

CHAPTER 4

In the aftermath of something huge, people often talk about the stand out moments. How clear something is in their memory.

For Sophia, the rest of the evening was a giant, gaping, empty hole in her memory. Kind of like how her heart felt.

So she felt pretty shocked when she woke up in a very masculine bedroom, smelling like cologne and something musky, sunlight pooling over her very clearly naked chest and a black waffle duvet tangled around her waist.

Her first thought: this wasn't Eliot's bedroom. Second: the bed sheets weren't the only thing she was tangled in.

An arm was thrown over her waist, and a leg was loosely entwined with hers. Both were very muscled, dusted finely with dark hair, and belonged to a man who she didn't know.

Well, fuck.

Untangling herself would likely wake the stranger, and Sophia was too ashamed to look at his face. She couldn't remember what he looked like, anyway.

Instead, she had the pleasure of lying in a stranger's bed, obviously having had sex — really good sex, if the ache in her core indicated anything —thinking about why this had happened in the first place.

Memories slowly trickled in. Eliot. Dinner. Breaking up. Shock, followed by pure, unadulterated, female rage. Things had definitely been broken, but Soph couldn't remember what. Hopefully the asshole's nose. Or at least his wine glass.

The reminder of his need for liquid courage to end their five year long relationship — two years of which she thought she was waiting for a ring — renewed her anger yet again.

"Damn coward," she breathed.

A soft sigh to her left made her stiffen, and she remembered that she wasn't alone. Soph didn't know what was worse: the fact that now she had to try to leave here (wherever that was) with whatever remained of her dignity (not likely to happen or remain intact), or the fact that she had just realised that this was the first person she'd ever been with aside from Eliot, in, like, ever.

And she didn't even remember it.

Groaning mentally, Sophia made her choice. Her dress was a vague lump on the floor, her panties and bra outside her field of vision. She didn't know which set she'd worn but it would be a damn shame if they ended up being her favourite pair.

Tensing, heart in her throat, she slipped her legs away from the man's and rolled out from his arm. A loud breathy sound had Sophia scared to look to see whether she had woken him, and gave her the motivation to move faster.

She may have made a series of bad decisions last night, but wearing a short silk slip dress was not one of them.

In seconds, she was acceptably covered, had found her purse, and managed to locate the front door relatively soundlessly.

It wasn't until she had ducked into a cab that Soph finally relaxed enough to check her phone. As expected, several missed calls and a variety of texts, most from Nef, some from Xander, and none from Eliot.

The implications of the last twenty four hours finally crashed into her. And once the tears started, she wasn't sure if she could stop.

Sophia could barely stand to look Nef in the eye. She sat on her friend's couch in the living room, wrapped in a soft blanket she could hardly feel.

Thankfully, Nef had witnessed her in dire situations before, and had acted faster than an emergency response team; Xander had been forced to retreat to their bedroom upstairs, a variety of chocolate packs were spread on the low coffee table, and Nef had provided choices of water, tea, coffee, juice, wine, or whisky.

Shifting in her seat, Soph tried to wrap her head around what Nef had told her.

Long story short: it was an Elle Woods situation, except instead of working towards the bar exam, Sophia had worked the local bar until she found someone random to have,

"And I quote," Nef said, "'hot, steamy, sex the likes of which Eliot could only dream about'."

Soph had to hand it to herself — her body felt sore in a way that could only mean she had succeeded. Still, that didn't stop the tsunami of guilt, self-loathing, and despair that had made its home in her chest.

Yes, she had certain... tastes in the bedroom. She wasn't very vocal about it, and hadn't actually participated in many of them before. There was a reason she didn't engage in her desires often, instead happy to go along with whatever Eliot had wanted to try. It was

— had been — good, and she'd felt plenty satisfied, but she didn't feel like it excused her from seeking out a stranger for revenge sex the second she got dumped. There was supposed to be a three month waiting period at least, right?

"I wasn't... drunk was I?" Soph felt her hands tremble as she snuck a glance at Nef.

"No, god no!" Her friend tossed her curls indignantly. "You think I'd ever let you get drunk and go home with someone? Or even talk to some random at a bar?"

Sophia let out a breath she didn't realise she had been holding.

"Honey, I'm no doctor, but this happened when your dad was first diagnosed, remember?"

Soph did remember — the aftermath, at least. The slow, eventual return of herself as she came to terms with what should have been a terminal diagnosis, and then the sheer miracle of her Dad's recovery and remission when she was thirteen. Even then, the doctors had told her she suppressed traumatic memories, leaving nothing behind but a black gaping emptiness.

Exactly like her 'memories' of last night.

Groaning loudly, she put down her empty glass of water and threw her head in her hands, long blonde waves falling over her face.

"I think I'm ready for the whisky, now." She muttered.

"Oh honey," Nef scooted closer on the couch, rubbing her back comfortingly. "I am so, so, sorry. No-one would ever have seen this coming. You don't deserve it one bit."

Soph hiccuped as tears threatened to overwhelm her again.

"Talk to me love," Nef's concerned voice turned softer as Soph was pulled into a hug.

In the comfort of her best friend's arms and her familiar cinnamon and citrus scent, Soph started to bawl again. Thank goodness she had already cried off most of her mascara on the ride over.

"I just," she got out in between sobs, "who do I text now? Who do I say good morning and goodnight to? Am I supposed to try the dating pool again? I'm not built to date!"

Her chest had started heaving uncontrollably, and she kept ranting as though a dam had broken.

"I thought he loved me just as much. I thought he was *proposing*. I feel so *stupid*, and *worthless*, and, and I can't help thinking that no one else will ever love me the way Eliot did, if this even counted as love at all considering he just dumped me. He wouldn't have dumped me if he loved me, right? God, I'm going to be alone forever aren't I."

A thought occurred to her, and Sophia almost threw up.

"Oh god, Nef. What if there's someone else?!"

Having patiently let Sophia spew her internal monologue, Nef was a good friend. She was even better when she immediately denied Soph's worst fear.

"Not a chance, Soph. He may be an idiot for losing you, but he's not cruel. He'd never hurt you like that."

"But he did hurt me." Soph's breathing was calming down.

"He did," Nef agreed softly. "But I've got you. Your friends have got you. You are so loved, and you're so amazing I don't even have all the words for it. But I guarantee you are not going to end up alone."

Sophia hummed sadly.

"Give it time, honey. I promise men will be tripping over themselves for you, and you don't have to do anything you're not comfortable with."

Too drained to continue the conversation, Soph leaned further into her friend and closed her eyes. Within seconds, she was fast asleep.

CHAPTER 5

"I'm so tired I want to die."

The muttered comment stemmed from a young twenty-something medical student to his friend, and although Zach remembered that feeling well, he was beyond that level of tired now and had no fucks left to spare.

"Mr Anderson, do I need to remind you we're in an oncology ward? Please refrain from using those comments until you're outside the hospital, please."

The student's face flushed. Ignoring the mumbled apologies, Zach surveyed the chart of the young girl sleeping in front of him. She was his last patient for the day, and as soon as he had grilled his students about her, he would finally be able to go home and sleep.

He loved his job. Normally. But it was only Monday, and today had seen too many Leukaemia patients. And too many bad prognoses. He wanted peace, quiet, and a few hours to eat whatever frozen meal he had left in his freezer while watching reruns of 'Friends' on TV.

Maybe some time to think about the other week's mind blowing hook up.

Zach wasn't one to normally sleep around. He didn't care if people did, but his tastes ran a certain way and he liked to be very selective with who he shared it with. On the rare occasions he found someone though, it was enough to fuel his fantasies for years.

It also didn't hurt that in the stranger's haste to leave, she had left a very pretty set of lingerie at his. He was no creep, so he had thrown them out immediately, but the image of her dripping in silk, the creamy lace panties slowly revealed along with long legs and a willowy figure, felt like it had been branded behind his eyes in a way his previous hookups had never been.

So his last week had been an exercise in self control, a constant stream of blinks that alternated between visions of hospital beds and a stunning blonde.

Finally, his shift ended. Zach dragged himself towards the car park, too tired to even change out of scrubs. He hadn't even made it past the ICU before a group of nurses descended upon him like sharks smelling blood, a chorus of hello's and questions about his plans for the evening echoing down the hall.

God, those nurses. Zach took a deep breath. They were great people, and lord knew they knew how to do their jobs well. But they were also some of the biggest gossips in the hospital, and Zach went to great lengths to keep his life private.

Bracing himself to politely but firmly exit the building, Zach's hopes were dashed when he saw Angelo, the oncology chief resident, determinedly charging towards him. Even though Zach technically ranked higher as attending physician, Angelo was often charged with passing along messages from their boss, Bridget, the head of department.

Basically, Zach's night was about to get a lot longer.

"Dr Hayes. Long shift?" Zach diplomatically ignored the slight smugness Angelo exuded.

"Always, Angelo. What's up?" Angelo bristled subtly at Zach's colloquialism. He always had been too uptight.

"Dr Hughes wants to see you. It's about that clinical trial application you submitted."

All of a sudden, Zach's fatigue seemed to disappear. Straightening, he cleared his throat. "She received my application?"

"Obviously, or I would be with patients right now instead of here with you." Angelo crossed his arms.

"I'll head over now. Thanks, Dr Reid."

Turning around, Zach speed walked back to the wards, heading to Bridget's office. This clinical trial would be huge if he got the grant for it. He didn't need to employ many others, just a medical researcher and a pharmacologist, one of whom he already had an agreement with — provided they received the grant.

Nerves bubbled up in his chest as he dodged patients and carts of equipment. The ethics forms were already completed, the consent documents were all printed and labelled, the methodology just needed some slight editing before it was fully ready to go, and all that was left was sending out recruitment advertisements.

If this worked, Zach would have actually done something good with his life. All those years of sacrifice, of study, of watching patients die because he didn't have the right drugs to give them. He would be able to finally save lives, not just give patients a good death.

His sister's voice was faint in the back of his head, whispering that he did save lives, that giving patients a good death could sometimes mean more than prolonging their time living in pain.

She was right, of course. But Zach knew that with this drug trial, he could do so much more for his patients.

Reaching Bridget's office, he knocked sharply. A professionally dressed brunette opened the door almost instantly, blinking at him through her sleek tortoiseshell frames.

"Hey Zach, I know your shift is finished but I figured you'd want to hear about your trial application immediately?"

"Thanks so much Bridget, the sooner the better!" He followed his boss to her small desk, sitting opposite her with the familiarity of long-time colleagues.

Bridget placed a clipboard of paper in front of him, before leaning back and smoothing her hair. "Long story short, it's been approved."

A breath rushed out of Zach, and he eagerly grabbed the folder and started flicking through it.

"Don't get too excited, Dr Hayes. We have one condition." Bridget was smiling though.

Of everyone at the hospital, she had always been the toughest — and the most understanding — of him. It was thanks to her mentorship that Zach was even interested in research, after doing his first year project with her researching a new technology for breast tumour detection.

"Any condition is fine! When do I have permission to start?" Zach was half here in the office, half thinking about booking the lab at their partner college before anyone else nabbed it.

"Dates depend on the condition. There's a medical scientist we employed a few years ago who's highly experienced with working with mice. She has a particular interest in oncology, and while her current project is looking at MS, she recently expressed to her supervisor an interest in applying for a PhD in clinical pharmacology. We'd like you to hire her, and have put her contact details — obtained with permission — in one of the forms you have there.

Now, before you go on your nepotism rant and how 'all doctors need to have contacts in the industry blah blah blah', I want to make it extremely clear that this was merit based. I've seen her work, and she's damn good at it. She's also a decent writer, which I'm sure you'll appreciate more than me." Bridget raised an eyebrow in faint amusement.

"Firstly, I wasn't going to say anything about nepotism or having to know other people to get ahead." He totally was. "Secondly, I trust your opinion."

Plus if she was a good writer...

Zach had always dreamt of publishing his research in a prominent scientific journal, but writing had never been his strong suit. He could collect the data and carry out experiments pretty well, but ask him to submit a succinct, polished report?

Not a chance in hell.

"I assume dates depend on her availability then?" Zach asked.

"And on the availability of whichever pharmacologist you're planning to hire. Do you have anyone in mind?"

"Finn said he's interested if the grant goes ahead."

"Dr Finn O'Connor? The guy from the pharmacy in the neuro ward?"

"That's the one."

"Good choice, I've heard he's good with the patients as well as the drugs." Bridget had stood up now and was hovering near the door, a clear hint that he should start leaving.

Zach wasn't insulted — standing up, he felt the familiar ache of a day spent on his feet. Leaving sounded good.

"Thanks again, Dr Hughes," Zach said. "I really appreciate your help and the grant."

"I know," Bridget smiled. "I'm excited to see the results. Your proposal has real potential here Zach."

The only thing that worried him as he reached the lockers and changed out of his scrubs was this new med sci woman Bridget had raved about. Working with someone he didn't know wouldn't be an issue; it was a normal part of his job, and it went for other doctors and patients alike. He just hoped this person would be able to start as soon as possible.

The sooner the trial was started, the sooner it ended, and the sooner Zach could get his work published and the drug out on the market under some ridiculously cheap licensing plan. It wouldn't quite be free for patients, but it should be pretty damn affordable. And affordable meant more lives saved, in and out of the wards.

Feeling lighter than he had all day at this thought, Zach finally made it to his car, grant forms in hand.

Step one, done. He'd worry about start dates tomorrow.

CHAPTER 6

Waking up in places she didn't recognise was becoming a habit for Sophia. Fortunately, the flimsy blinds let in enough sunlight to emphasise the sickeningly cute engagement photos on the opposite wall, reminding her that she was on Nef and Xander's couch.

Wiping sleep from her eyes, Soph wracked her brain for why she was still at her friend's place. Oh yeah, because she couldn't face going back to her apartment which was full of half of he-who-must-not-be-named's stuff. She should probably do something about that. Especially after the email she had gotten late last night.

Footsteps sounded in the hallway and a yeti in a nightgown appeared. Yawning, the yeti plodded her way to the coffee machine, her mop of curls seemingly defying gravity.

"Don't give me that guilty look." The yeti mumbled. "Xander and I are fine with you staying however long you want. Plus, I'm happy to help clear out your place when you're ready. We can have a bonfire night and burn the asshole's hoodies."

Soph flopped back onto the couch pillows, torn between a groan and a smile. She knew that even after caffeine, Nef would still follow through on her violent promise the second Soph said the word.

Her smile won out, along with her growling stomach. "I might take you up on that. Make me a cup too?"

Nef nodded and got out a second mug, dumping three spoonfuls of sugar into her own and none into Soph's. Nef had always had a sweet tooth, and the familiarity of it calmed Sophia enough to bring up what had kept her up so late last night.

"So uh… last night, I, uh, got a job offer." Twisting the wool blanket between her fingers, Soph waited for Nef's response, determinedly fixing her eyes on her feet.

"Is this the one at the university? Congratulations!" Nef was halfway through her coffee and already sounded more human. It helped that her hair was starting to point more towards the floor than the walls.

"Kind of…" Sophia pulled herself into a cross legged position and accepted the mug Nef proffered.

"Soph. Stop teasing. Spit it out."

Soph took a long sip of her coffee, enjoying the way her friend's eyes narrowed.

"Ok ok, relax babes. I just woke up." Soph relented at last. "So you know how I applied for that PhD? I didn't get it — *yet* — but my current supervisor knows someone who works at our partner hospital, in the oncology ward. They've asked me to be part of a small clinical trial for a new chemo drug."

Nef whooped and threw an arm around Soph, her coffee tipping dangerously to the side.

"Wait, wait!" Soph returned the hug, grinning. "The best part is, if this gets published, then it practically guarantees me the PhD position!"

For the first time since *that* night, Soph felt a flutter of excitement as she said the words aloud. Doing her doctorate in clinical pharmacology had been a distant dream since her Dad's cancer journey, but she hadn't properly considered it until a few months ago, when she had mentioned something in passing to Joanna, her supervisor.

She hadn't told Eliot at the time. He had known about her goal, but... it didn't really feel like something concrete, and she hadn't wanted to jinx herself by saying anything.

Now, she supposed, he'd never know. She didn't really know what to think of that yet.

Nef nudged her knee with her own. "So? Did you say yes?"

"I only got the email last night," Soph said with a sigh.

"So naturally, you've already said yes."

Soph sighed again. "I said yes."

Xander chose that moment to walk in, immediately clamping his hands over his ears as the two girls squealed with excitement on the couch.

"What did I miss?" Like Nef, he made a beeline to the coffee machine. They really were made for each other.

"I got a new job!" Sophia said jubilantly.

"Congratulations!" Xander smiled at her over his cup, and Nef walked over to wrap her arms around him. "What's the role?"

"I'm part of a small research team for a new chemo drug trial. The contract doesn't specify anything aside from that there'll only be three of us, it will likely go for over a year, and that the first author is an oncology attendant who will call me to discuss further details within the week."

"Nice. I'm excited to hear more when you start." Nef whispered something to Xander, and they fell into their own little bubble, leaving Soph to finish her coffee quietly.

She'd tell her Dad about the job when she saw him next, probably tomorrow night for dinner or something. Eliot should be awake now though.

Jolting, Soph reminded herself again that Eliot was no longer an option. Chewing the inside of her cheek, she realised that he hadn't even been the first person she had wanted to tell. Was that a sign that their relationship hadn't been as good as she had thought? Maybe the breakup really was her fault.

No. This was a bad line of thought to go down. It had only been a week, and while she had stopped crying multiple times during the day, she still went to sleep with puffy eyes and a clogged nose. It was what she liked to call 'progress'.

Pushing thoughts of Eliot to the back of her mind was unfortunately not an option today. The new job meant higher pay — not by much, but by enough that she could move somewhere better than her shitty studio apartment. Soph had been saving for ages to... well, to move in with Eliot. At least now she could afford someplace of her own, a fresh start away from her room stained with unwanted memories. And she could give Nef back her space and privacy with her fiancé.

That meant facing her apartment today. And getting ready for a bonfire night.

***

Several hours and several burnt hoodies later, Soph was back on Nef's couch, the hallway stuffed with various cardboard boxes full of her worldly possessions. She hadn't bothered asking Eliot about handing over her things she'd left at his — he could burn them, for all she cared now. Sure, she'd miss her favourite sex toys (and she doubted her bonfire routine would work on them) but, as Nef had assured her, she would find "better toys and better boys, hopefully in that order.".

On the bright side, her landlord had let her break her lease early, and Xander had asked his friend Asim to keep an eye out for any local apartments he saw going for rent. To make today better, the first author — Zach — had texted her today with contract details and to organise a start date, so she finally had her budget set.

Soph had nearly snorted her water out of her nose when she saw the stipend the hospital was offering her. She'd done well enough over the years, putting in overtime and weekends when the mice weren't cooperating, but this was a whole new level of academia, one she hadn't realised she could reach. It definitely left her a bit smug.

How's that for a promotion, huh Eliot, she thought to herself as she surfed the web for one bedroom places.

Muttering obscenities under her breath as she aggressively searched real estate sites, Soph almost didn't notice her phone dinging.

HI SOPHIA, it read. *DR O'CONNOR IS ALSO AVAILABLE TO START ON FRIDAY. WE WILL SEE YOU AT 9AM AT THE JACOBS MEDICAL CENTRE. THE ADDRESS HAS BEEN LINKED BELOW.*

Sophia dramatically forced herself to pump a fist in the air. Success! Fake it til' you make it, and all that crap. New job, soon a new place, and then a new start that hopefully wouldn't feel as hollow as the thought did.

Well. If this Zach guy was anything like how he sounded in his texts — efficient, professional, and boring — then she'd have plenty of work to do soon to keep her distracted.

CHAPTER 7

Zach had never felt his blood and his professionalism leave his body so quickly. The blood was a lie, actually. It didn't so much as leave his body as drain entirely to a very specific organ.

He shifted discreetly in his chair as the woman in front of him kept talking to Finn. Her blonde waves cascaded down her back, glinting in the light that streamed through the broad window in his third floor office.

Sophia Adkins was acting extremely professionally, to her favour. It was as though she didn't even recognise him. While their one night stand may have been a few weeks ago now, Zach wasn't sure if he was relieved that she wasn't making their new relationship as colleagues awkward, or if he was insulted that he'd left so little an impression on her.

Sophia glanced questioningly at him and he quickly forced himself to relax his jaw. If she could be professional about this, he could too.

Pushing away memories of the blonde beauty riding him, long nails scraping gently over his nipples with just enough pain to keep him on edge, Zach crossed his legs again and leant forward to catch the end of Sophia and Finn's conversation.

"— if there's anything you want to change, just let me know and I can have a finalised timeline by next week." Sophia spoke with a quiet but strong tone of authority.

Zach cut in quickly. "Ethics has already been approved, including for using the mice. Let me know what lab you'd prefer to use and I can set it up for whatever time works best for you."

Sophia smiled politely, dipping her chin in thanks. Finn was scribbling madly on a notepad, probably making a list of tasks that he would need considered in the planning.

"I know everyone will be busy with their own tasks and other roles until we start our face to face component with participants, but should we schedule a consistent time for us all to meet and update each other?"

"Mondays, eight o'clock," Finn mumbled distractedly at Sophia. The man was a good friend of his, but he really did have a one track mind sometimes. And a work ethic that put people to shame all the time.

"Nine o'clock," Zach countered smoothly, chest warming as Sophia shot him another smile, this one with a hint of gratefulness.

Something in his chest seemed to... wake up at that smile. He chose to ignore it.

They kept discussing logistics for another half hour before deciding to wrap things up. Zach had to admit to himself, he had been a little worried about Sophia's credentials, and while that worry had compounded when he recognised her, she had really impressed him with her obvious competency.

The fact that she was gorgeous, confident, but also clearly intelligent and kind as well, was not helping the crush that he had developed over the course of their meeting.

The employee handbook and code of ethics crowded his head as they started to pack up their notes and laptops, but it wasn't enough to stop him from voicing a bad decision.

"Sophia?" He called as she reached the door, hair swaying enticingly. "A few of the staff are getting drinks at Kitsch Bar tonight. You — and Finn — are welcome to join, get to know the team here."

Finn's eyebrows shot up as he finally started paying attention to the people in the room rather than the task at hand. Pointedly ignoring the way the other doctor's eyes narrowed as he glanced between him and Sophia,

Zach kept his own gaze focused on the enigma in front of him.

"That sounds nice. What time?" Sophia spoke after a brief hesitation.

"Any time from seven." It was a damn shame the tightness in his throat couldn't be attributed to his peanut allergy. Maybe there was something in the air. Definitely wasn't nerves as he waited for this woman's response to a completely platonic colleague catch up.

She nodded slightly, and Zach let a grin slide loose in response.

"I'll be there too," Finn spoke up as Sophia left the room. "Because my best friend Zach invited me. Because I definitely did not just get roped into this as a ploy for you to semi-ask out some new girl."

"Oh fuck off," Zach mumbled, gathering his folders and pager.

"You're welcome," Finn smirked as he went back to his notebook. "See you at seven, lover boy."

So Zach was definitely efficient and professional. What he was not, however, was boring.

Sophia worried her bottom lip between her teeth as she approach Kitsch Bar, fashionably twenty minutes past seven. She had changed back at Nef's, swapping her cream no-nonsense blouse and black trousers for a modest but more playful blue long sleeve dress.

She had also made a quick detour on her way to the bar.

Zach was, of course, already there. He did strike her as the punctual type, but Soph was glad that she would know one person at least. Two, if you count Finn — which she didn't because he was in the back corner of the wide booth, somehow *still* scribbling in his notebook.

"Did you," Zach started as she came towards him and the older woman by his side, "Did you cut your hair?"

Her hand drifted to her collarbone, where her previously straight blonde hair was now in soft layered waves.

"Is it that obvious?" She smiled self-consciously. The decision hadn't exactly been spontaneous. Like any girl post-break up, she was desperate for a physical change, a sign to show herself that things were different now but in a way that she could control.

Soph hadn't expected the extreme satisfaction that came when her long strands were chopped, though. The weight was literally lifted off her shoulders — plus the fact that her hair had been one of Eliot's favourite features gave her an extra dose of smugness.

"It looks nice," Zach was staring at her with an unreadable expression. Something about him seemed suddenly really familiar...

"You must be Sophia," the woman next to him cut in, holding out a perfectly manicured hand. "I'm Bridget. It's nice to have you at the centre."

"Thank you, it's nice to meet you. Do you work with Zach on the wards?"

"Honey, I *am* the wards." Zach choked as Bridget winked. "Oh, that's mine!"

Bridget ducked away to the bar to grab her cocktail, and Zach cleared his throat.

"So that's Dr Bridget Hughes, my boss."

"Makes sense that a woman like her is in charge around here," Soph grinned. "She seems fun."

"Only when out of scrubs."

"And is this what you do for fun? Drinks after work?"

"Among other things," Zach's voice seemed to lower, the sound doing something funny to her stomach.

"Oh?" She had nothing eloquent to say right now. Not even a single drink, but her stomach was doing some weird fluttery thing.

"Do you... remember that night a few weeks ago?"

Wow, he had really pretty eyes. Nice eyelashes. Some flecks of green.

Wait. "What night a few weeks ago?"

He frowned, and Sophia felt like she was missing something important.

"That night? When we *first* met...?"

She had seen eyes that pretty once before, hadn't she? Recognition set ice running through her veins.

Oh fucking fucking *fuck*.

CHAPTER 8

"Oh my *god*," Sophia groaned, cheeks burning. "That was you?"

Zach's face dropped. "Please tell me you weren't drunk that night. You told me you hadn't drunk anything."

"Oh gosh, no, nothing like that!" Zach pressed a hand to his chest, colour slowly returning to his face. Dropping her head in her hands, Sophia let a small shriek slip out from behind her clenched jaw.

"What a mess. I am so, so, sorry Zach. If I had realised earlier, I never would have taken this job or put you in this position!"

"Why are you apologising? Neither of us had any idea. I mean, I recognised you at our first meeting this morning, but I figured you were being professional and were just pretending to not know who I was."

Wincing, Sophia stepped towards the booth next to them and slumped into a seat. Zach followed, sliding opposite her.

"For both our peace of minds, that night was completely consensual. I just…" Sucking in a breath, she took a second to debate how much she should tell Zach.

Fuck it. She'd already slept with him, and now they were working together. May as well go all in.

"I have a tendency to suppress memories after something…traumatic happens to me. And no, sleeping with you was not traumatic," Sophia shot an amused glare at him as Zach smirked. "My boyfriend of five years dumped me that night. While we were on a date."

"The *fuck*?" Zach burst out indignantly.

"Oh it gets better," Sophia held up a hand. "I thought he was proposing to me that night. I had waited for this night for *two years*, since he first asked me to go ring shopping together. So yeah. I did what many self-respecting women do after that — headed to a bar with friends and looked for a distraction. When I woke up the next day, I was, well, embarrassed, and angry, and heartbroken, and I ran home before I really saw you properly."

"I don't know what to say. What a dick!" Zach was clenching his fists so hard over the table that Sophia could count the veins in his forearm. Not that she was noticing, or anything. Especially not after connecting her anonymous night of passion with the man (kinda her boss?) sitting in front of her.

"There's nothing really to say. It sucked. I'm trying to move on. But I promise it was just a one night thing, and I never ever do that normally, and I promise I won't let this interfere with our work."

Sophia blew out a deep breath. Somehow, admitting all of this to Zach made her feel lighter. It was nice seeing an almost stranger get this worked up on her behalf.

Zach was shaking his head. Surprising her, he reached over the table and took her hand in his.

"I'm really sorry that happened to you, Sophia," he murmured. His brown eyes swirled with sympathy, but not pity. Thank god. "I wish I had known. I would have —"

"Would have treated me differently?" Sophia's lips twisted.

"I was going to say, 'would have tried to make it more memorable for you, at least. God knows how injured my pride was to hear you actually didn't remember me." Zach winked, and Sophia felt her stomach swoop.

She let out a soft snort, relaxing back against the booth's hard wooden surface.

"Anyway, I'm just really embarrassed — about my ex, and about this whole situation with... Us. Can we start over? Please?"

"Hmm." Zach drummed his fingers against the table, no longer touching her. "I don't really want to start over. I like you, Sophia. As a friend, to be clear. I mean, I'd like us to be friends. How about we just put this all behind us?"

Shoving down the slight disappointment she felt at being reduced to 'just friends', Sophia smiled and nodded. She was in no mindset for a relationship right now. Maybe not for a long, long time.

"In the spirit of friendship, I also feel obligated to share an embarrassing story with you. You know, to balance out the power dynamic of knowing your deepest darkest secret." Zach's smile was edging on sarcastic, and Soph leaned into this new relationship dynamic.

"Please do, Z. God knows it's always smart to air your dirty laundry in a public bar in front of your coworkers."

Zach flushed, and Sophia cringed. "Sorry, are nicknames too soon? It just kind of slipped out."

"No, I like it." There was a funny look on his face Soph couldn't decipher. "What do your friends call you? Only fair I give you one back."

"Mostly just Soph. Nothing special."

"You're nothing if not special," Zach said quietly.

She didn't know how to respond to that. Or to the heavy layer of silence that descended over them at his statement. Zach was quick to break it though.

"I'll think of a better one soon. Anyway, my embarrassing story. So for context, my parents are American, but I was born in Australia when they were there for work, and we moved from Sydney to San Diego when I was five. This is important, because at my going-away party, something terrible happened. Get ready, cause this is really traumatic and has scarred me in ways that aren't physically visible."

He took a deep breath, and Soph leaned forward in anticipation.

"An ibis stole my birthday cake."

She blinked. That had not been even remotely close to what she thought he might say.

"What's an ibis?"

"A fucking menace, is what it is. A stupid, white, long-beaked bird that steals children's cake."

"You poor baby," Sophia crooned, holding back laughter. "That's not even embarrassing."

"I was a poor baby! A poor four year old with no cake on the day before I was leaving to a new country. Not that I really comprehended what was going on, cause I was four. But that was a core memory!"

Sophia couldn't help it anymore. As laughter burst from her lips, Zach joined in, and soon the two of them were shaking soundlessly in their booth at the far side of the bar.

As Sophia continued to tease him gently about the ibis incident in between meeting the rest of his co-workers (who had slowly trickled in over the last hour),

Zach struggled to keep the murderous rage he felt off his face at the knowledge that Sophia had been dumped so brutally by her ex. What idiot would dump *her*?

He'd only spent a total of four hours with her today (the one night stand didn't count, now that he knew she didn't have clear memories of it) but he already knew she was a fucking treasure. The man must have been clinically insane.

Pushing aside thoughts of violence, Zach instead spent the next hour mingling with his colleagues and making sure he kept chatting with Sophia when things got quiet.

Being friends with her already felt so natural. Things should have felt awkward, given all that had already happened between them. Instead, being around her, joking with her, felt right in a way he hadn't felt in years.

It was a shame he had lied about wanting to just be friends.

No, Zach thought to himself. You saw the way she reacted when talking about her ex. She's in no place to get romantically involved with someone, especially not this soon after a five year relationship. You'd be a jerk for trying.

A hand on his shoulder snapped him out of his thoughts.

"I'm heading home," Bridget was saying. "Enjoy your weekend, and don't forget you're on the nightshift on Monday."

Zach groaned as his boss left the bar. Nightshifts were hell, but at least they paid well. More people started to leave, despite — or perhaps because of — a flood of teenagers entering the venue.

"Really reminds me how old I am," a soft voice said from behind him. "I remember when I used to start my nights at ten. Now I'm ending them."

Turning to Sophia, Zach was again struck by the way the light played in her now-short hair, a blend of yellows with some mousy brown strands peaking through. It reminded him of a

"Sunflower."

"What?" Sophia glanced up from where she was pulling out a soft looking cardigan from her handbag.

"That's my nickname for you. Sunflower."

Sophia blushed, a delicious pink spreading over her cheekbones, making a tiny smattering of freckles under her left eye stand out. Shoving down the desire to lick each one, Zach pulled his phone out of his pocket to check the time.

"I'm going to end my night here too. How are you getting home?"

"I was just planning to walk to the station. I'm staying with a friend until I find a new apartment."

"I'll walk with you."

They fell into a companionable silence as they left the bar, walking close enough to occasionally bump shoulders.

"Are you looking for a new place because you were living with your ex?" As Sophia's gaze shot towards him, he winced. "Sorry, I don't want to pry if you're not comfortable."

"You're not prying. But no, I wasn't living with him. Maybe that should have been the first sign things weren't heading where I thought they were."

Zach stayed silent, giving Sophia the space to say as much or as little as she needed to. She sighed, the sound so dejected that he wanted to wrap her in his arms and hold her until she never felt a need to make that sound again.

"Actually, now I'm thinking of it, there was definitely more than one red flag. This job? I'm doing it to help me get into my dream PhD program. I've wanted to study cancer pharmaceutics forever, but I never really talked about it with Eliot."

Eliot. What a stupid name. Made sense if he was stupid enough to give up this woman.

"Why didn't you talk about it with him if it's been your dream forever?" Zach searched Sophia's face as a sad smile played at her mouth.

"I brought it up, a few times the first few years we were dating. He... he told me that he thought I'd be better off behind a lab bench rather than being an academic. Said the field would be too cut-throat for me, and would take up too much of my time if I was always busy studying."

Sophia frowned, eyes lighting with anger. "Wow. I really should have seen the signs sooner, shouldn't I."

"He was an asshole, Sunflower." her eyes shot to Zach's, and he let her see the determination and sincerity in them as he continued. "He was an asshole, and you don't have to worry about him now."

She smiled slightly, but it still wasn't enough for Zach. This beautiful, smart, funny woman had become what he'd consider a close friend in the span of one night. And if Zach knew one thing about himself with certainty, it was that he'd always, always, go to the mat for his friends.

"Hey, I have an idea. To kind of get back at him, but also to help you get that PhD."

"Oh yeah?" Sophia's smile was warmer this time.

"Want to be co-author of this paper with me?"

CHAPTER 9

The rest of the weekend passed in a blur. As was tradition for their friend group, Soph, Nef, Zara, and Lilah had gone out on Saturday night to celebrate Sophia's new job and potential co-authorship. She could have kissed Zach for the offer — for what it would mean for her future as well as for her past.

In another life, where she had been single for more than a month, Zach might have been the perfect guy for her. But in this life, all he could be was a good friend. And that was more than ok with Sophia. Goodness knew she wasn't ready for more romance. Definitely one day, if anyone was ever interested. But not for a while.

In good news though, thoughts of Eliot were becoming less frequent and less tear-inducing. She could listen to Taylor Swift again without bawling, and didn't feel an urge to break plates whenever Legally Blonde popped up on TV.

For a five year relationship ending only a month ago, she sure was doing better than she thought at this stage.

Humming along to 'Long Live', Sophia pottered around the kitchen making herself a pre-dinner snack of vanilla ice cream with crushed pistachios. With Nef and Xander out on a date, she had the house to herself for once. It was a novelty she hoped would soon become a reality once she found a new place.

Plopping herself down onto the couch, she pulled up the real estate website on her laptop for the millionth time. Music was still blaring for her phone as she scrolled past various rentals, and time flew as she sent in a few applications for some decent one-bedrooms nearby.

It wasn't until two hours later that Sophia bothered to check her phone and pause the music.

"That's a lot of messages," she murmured to herself. No one ever blew up her phone like this.

Sliding open her group chat with the girls — titled 'Dylan O'Brien's Sluts' — she wrinkled her brow at the slew of capital letters that crowded her vision.

Nef: *DON'T LOOK AT INSTAGRAM!*

Nef: *SOPHIA*

Nef: *SOPH DON'T OPEN INSTA*

Nef: *!!!!!!!*

Lilah: *Oh honey that's awful, call us whenever you need!*

Zara: *oh SHIT*

Zara: *I'm gonna kill him*

Nef: *Me too*

Nef: *Soph call us*

Ice rushed through her veins even as her cheeks grew hot. Was Nef ok? What had happened?

Trembling, Soph decided to open Instagram.

Before she could, Nef's photo popped up on screen, green phone button obscuring the social media app.

"Nef! Oh my god, are you ok? What's wrong?" Sophia sat up straighter on the couch, putting her friend on speaker.

"Oh thank god," Nef sounded puffed. "You haven't opened Insta."

"I was about to but then you called. What's going on?"

"Just," Nef hesitated. "Don't open Insta. I'm coming over right now. Please promise you'll wait for me!"

Surely whatever it was couldn't be this bad.

"Ok fine. I promise. But you're scaring me."

"It's ok, it's gonna be fine. I promise it'll be fine. Just wait for me. I'll be there in ten!"

The line cut out, and Sophia slumped back in her seat, adrenaline pumping through her. What on earth was going on?

***

It was definitely that bad.

Zara, Lilah, and Nef were squished on either side of Soph on the couch, surrounded by blankets and emergency provisions such as vodka, Chinese takeout, and liquorice bullets.

Sophia hadn't touched any of it since they had opened Instagram.

Her friends chattered softly around her, but she couldn't hear what they were saying. She could barely feel Nef's hand rubbing comforting circles on her back, or Zara's warm hand in hers.

The only thing registering was that *fucking* photo.

Eliot, looking perfect as always with his sandy blond hair and full lips and his linen shirt like he was on the set of Mama Mia.

Eliot, holding a shorter, willowy woman with a pouty smile and perfectly straightened, waist length brown hair.

Except holding wasn't quite the right word. *Embracing*, maybe. *Canoodling. Cradling.*

Eliot moving on was a thousand direct punches to her gut.

She could have recovered from that. Hadn't she just been thinking about how she could move on in a few more months or years? Hell, she'd technically moved on the night of the breakup, physically at least.

Regardless, Sophia knew she could have recovered from that. What she couldn't recover from, though, was this new woman's stupidly perfect manicured fingers, which were splayed out in front of the camera in front of their stupid smiling faces, with a ring on it.

Sophia's ring, actually.

Yep. That gorgeous, specifically chosen for her by Eliot, high-set cushion cut two carat diamond with a diamond-studded gold band was sitting perfectly in frame, like Sophia's own personal Hell. One month after he had dumped her and their five year relationship down the drain.

She didn't think she could recover from that.

Being on the night shift as an attending was infinitely better than when Zach had been a medical student. For one, it meant that he only had to be at the hospital if he got paged. Which meant that unless he was paged, he could be wherever he wanted.

Right now, he was back at Kitsch Bar with Finn and Angelo, who had decided to dial back the asshole energy for tonight. There wasn't a chance in hell he was drinking while on call, but being around friends would help keep him awake without caffeine — a habit he was trying to quit.

"You know you can sleep until you're paged, right?" Angelo cocked an eyebrow as Zach smothered another yawn.

"I know," he responded.

"Zach's white saviour complex means he refuses to sleep while on call." Finn looked up from his notebook for a split second, naturally only paying attention to the conversation to roast him.

"I sleep," Zach said defensively. "Sometimes."

When he crashed because he didn't realise how tired he was. But his friends didn't need to know that, or know about how the thought of passing out and missing a page scared him enough to keep him up.

Finn and Angelo grumbled their disbelief but went back to their beers and the soccer game on the overhead screen.

A loud peal of laughter through the bar's open door distracted Zach from the game. Turning in his seat, he saw a flash of blonde hair, and Sophia's face came into view. Raising a hand to wave, Zach then noticed the man next to her, standing far too close for comfort.

Was she... on a date?

He tracked their pathway to a small table near the front window, on the same side of the bar as him and his friends. If she looked away from this guy for one second, she'd notice him. Not that he wanted her to notice him. They were just friends, after all. Very recently friends.

Torn between not wanting to interrupt her date and the weird tingling in his stomach urging him to do something drastic, Zach decided on a third option: spy pathetically from his seat as he sipped his glass of water.

Unfortunately, the next hour passed without any clue as to how the date was going. At least his pager remained silent, and he could continue his creepy vigil uninterrupted.

Ready to turn back to the game and force himself to ignore Sophia, the scraping of her chair as she stood up had him turning back towards her.

She looked exquisite. A white pencil skirt and short sleeved yellow blouse only reinforced that Zach had nicknamed her correctly. Dragging his eyes to her face, though, he frowned. Sophia's smile was wide, but looked a little... strained. And her hands clenched on the back of her chair were white knuckled. Zach would give good money that her blood pressure was probably through the roof right now, but he had no idea what they were saying to each other over the din of the crowd.

Suddenly, she turned on her heel and stalked towards the back of the bar, power walking down the brick hallway that blocked the patron's view of the bathrooms.

Unable to stop himself, Zach followed her.

CHAPTER 10

The second he rounded the corner of the dim hall, Zach knew he had miscalculated.

Sophia stood directly in front of him, hands on hips and a smile spelling trouble.

"You missed a great goal, Z," she smirked. "Seemed a bit distracted."

The Sophia in front of him was not the same woman from the bar last week. It was the woman he had taken home with him all those weeks ago.

Taking a deep breath, Zach steeled himself. You're just friends, remember? And she's still clearly not over her ex, no matter the fact she's on a date tonight. Just friends. No slipping up here, even if the look in her eye…

Clearing his throat, Zach slid his hands into the pockets of his jeans.

"I wanted to say hi, but I didn't want to interrupt."

"Next time, please interrupt." Sophia drew out the please, popping the 'p'. "The only reason I came to the bathroom was to try escape through a window. A stupid idea, I know."

"Mission Impossible style, I like it." Zach grinned.

"More like runaway bride style. It was that, or commit murder."

"So violent. What did the poor man do to deserve it?"

Sophia's hand moved to tug on a short curl that was falling out of a bobby pin.

"The 'poor man' called me some very choice words that I'm going to choose not to repeat. Had some very interesting insights into what he thought I should be doing with my life."

It was Zach's turn to feel physically violent. "I take it none of those insights had anything to do with STEM?"

Sophia laughed sadly. "That's what I get for trying to boost my ego with a tinder date."

"Yikes." Zach winced dramatically. "The universal date app mood booster attempt. Been there."

"No, you haven't," Sophia smiled at him.

"No, I haven't," he acquiesced. "But only because I've been told I'm too old for dating apps."

Sophia laughed again, and Zach realised how much closer she had gotten. His back was almost against the wall, and if she stepped a little closer, maybe he could finally work out what her perfume was.

Her eyes dipped to his mouth, and Zach's breaths turned heavy. This was too close. Too far away from being 'just friends'.

"Do you still think about that night?" She whispered.

It didn't take a genius to know which night she was talking about.

Lie, lie, lie, a voice in his head was yelling.

"Every day, Sunflower" Zach rumbled, the truth coming unbidden.

'Just friends' shattered into a million pieces as they crashed together, Sophia's hands in his hair and her soft, slim body pressed against his chest.

Groaning, Zach squeezed her waist, her ass, moving his hands up to her face to kiss her deeper, harder. God, he never did repeats with the people he had one night stands with. That was the whole point of a one night stand. But he couldn't lie to himself that he hadn't been craving her taste, her lips, since the moment he realised who she was at their first meeting.

With surprising strength, Sophia shoved him back against the bricks, the cold rough material catching on the cotton of his navy t-shirt. Her hand dipped to his belt, and she nipped his earlobe lightly.

"Is this ok, Z?"

"Yes!" He managed to grate out as he fisted the hair at the nape of her neck, stealing her mouth again. His belt came loose, and then Sophia's hand was under his briefs.

If this is what Sophia's hand felt like after just over a month, Zach was almost scared about how good her mouth, or — please, god — her pussy will feel like around him again.

A good kind of scared, the kind that brings an edge of pain, just enough to force him to dance on the precipice of finishing.

The kind of pain he craves.

The kind Sophia was giving him, without a hint of judgement.

"Harder," Zach gasped as Sophia squeezed lightly. She obliged, sharp nails pricking gently at the underside of his swollen member.

"Fuck, yes, Sunflower. As hard as you want. You're in control here, baby." He was babbling, but the way Sophia let out a small noise and pressed closer seemed to indicate she was enjoying this as much as he was.

Was it possible she craved control as much as he craved giving it up?

The sensations were already getting close to being too much. The scrape of her nails under his shirt as her other hand dragged down his chest, over a nipple. The tickle of Sophia's breath on his neck, and the wet, slow drag of her tongue as she licked up the curve of his neck.

He couldn't stop the way he was thrusting into her hand, staccato beats that she matched beat for beat with a rough twist of her palm. Zach didn't think that he had ever felt friction like this before.

More. He craved everything his Sunflower was willing to give, everything she allowed him to have and everything she wanted to withhold.

"You going to come for me, baby?" Sophia punctuated her statement with a gentle nip of his bottom lip, moving her hand even faster. "You going to let go right here, in this hallway where anyone could walk past, just because I say so?"

Yes. No. Yes. Wait.

What was he doing? Zach had only come over to see if Soph was ok after that date. She had just only recently told him that she had been heartbroken so viciously that he was ready to shatter his Hippocratic Oath. And now he was letting her get him off in some back-alley bathroom hall?

"Wait a sec, Sunflower," Zach ground out, forcing his hips to stop moving.

Sophia stopped immediately, backing away a step and breathing hard.

"Oh god, Zach, did I go too far? I'm so so sorry —"

"No no no you're fine, you're absolutely fine! I didn't mean it like that. That was fucking incredible. I just," Zach paused, trying to think how to best word this.

Dragging a hand over his faint stubble, he continued.

"I feel like I'm taking advantage of you. I didn't come check on you because I was looking for this, for some kind of reward."

"You think this was a reward? Like you're my white knight coming to my rescue?" Sophia cocked an eyebrow.

Oooh, Zach knew he had screwed up now. What was worse though, this? Or letting Sophia finish what they had started?

"...No?" Her face didn't change. Only he could have turned this into a lose-lose scenario.

"Zach." Her voice became a dangerous purr. "Let me make it exceptionally clear that I'm not a damsel in distress. I appreciate your help, I really do. You're a good man. But this? This has nothing to do with your hero complex."

Sophia reached out and roughly palmed him again through his still-open zipper, sending white sparks into his field of vision.

"I know," Zach managed to gasp out. "Sophia, god I want you..."

She leant forward, a mischievous glint sparking behind her eyes.

Squeezing his own eyes shut, Zach ripped the bandaid off.

"But I don't want you like this. I don't do relationships unless you're all in, and you're definitely in no position to be all in right now."

Sophia looked like he had thrown a bucket of water over her head. "Wait, are you really choosing now to decide what's best for me? How do you know I don't want just sex?"

"I didn't mean it like that!"

"You haven't meant a lot of things like that tonight, apparently."

"Sunflower, listen to me." Zach sucked in a calming breath and stood at his full height. He would never use his size against anyone, especially not this petite female who he admired and craved in equal measures, but a thrill went through him anyway when she squared her shoulders to somehow still look down her nose at him.

She had nothing to fear. With him, she would always be in control.

"Just sex is fine, normally. We've been there, done that." They smirked at each other.

"But you've just come out of a five year relationship. AND you just had one of the world's worst Tinder dates. God help me, the things I've been dreaming of doing to you... I couldn't forgive myself if I let that happen right now."

"Is my newly single status all that's stopping you?"

"Along with the fact that we're now working together contractually for at least a year."

"Don't tell me you're scared of the HR department."

"I'm always scared of the HR department. But I'm also scared that if we go any further, I'll lose your friendship. And that's more important to me right now."

She seemed speechless at that.

"So, to be clear, you really do want to be just friends?" She sounded only slightly incredulous, to her credit.

I'll be whatever you want me to be, Sunflower.

The words almost rolled off his tongue, but Zach held them back.

Wrong timing. Wrong person.

Zach knew he was a ridiculously monogamous man. He hated sharing. And the second he started a relationship with someone, his heart would inevitably get involved. Unfortunately, more often than not, his partners never wanted to explore his kinks except as one-off experiments. So until he found someone who shared his kinks AND his desire to be committed long-term, he wouldn't put himself in the firing line.

"Yes," he swallowed. "Just friends."

"Well, 'just friend', you may want to do up your zipper before we go back to the bar."

Amusement, relief, and disappointment simultaneously flooded Zach's veins as Sophia seamlessly adapted to their new boundaries.

Just friends. Surely it would hurt less than being something more.

The beeping of his pager going off saved him from thinking about how wrong he knew he would be.

CHAPTER 11

"I know I'm risking bodily harm by bringing this up, but can I at least ask what prompted... you know." Zach waggled his eyebrows suggestively as he leaned against her lab bench as Sophia carefully packed up her equipment for the night.

Although they had spent today in her lab rather than Zach's eerily sterile office, the man was still dressed distractingly in dark blue scrubs with his stethoscope draped around his neck. With his intense gaze and ever-present dimple, Soph had to admit she could understand why doctors always held so much appeal to her friends.

Soph had to give it to him. She knew this was long overdue, but he at least managed to wait the entire rest of the week until he cracked and brought up Monday night. It also helped that it was nine in the evening the next Monday, and though she, Zach, and Finn spent most late evenings working together, privacy was a rare commodity in the bustling medical centre.

Sipping her fourth mug of coffee — the words 'you know what gets on my nerves? Myelin!' stamped in red over the front — Sophia tried to stall her response.

"You're clearly stalling." Zach leant forward, arms crossed.

His biceps bunched up deliciously, and Sophia had a vivid flash of biting down on said arms as he —

Nope. Not going there.

Just friends.

Chewing on her lip, Sophia made a sound crossed between a growl and a whine.

"Do we have to talk about this?" She pouted exaggeratedly. "I thought this was all water under the bridge?"

Zach waved a hand absently, almost hitting the fake plant she kept on the corner of her bench (because real plants risk lab contamination). The clatter of the rattling plastic plant caused Finn to jump in the corner he was inhabiting, bringing the amount of times he had looked up from his notebook tonight to six.

Exchanging knowing looks, Sophia decided to relent slightly. "It's complicated."

"Not an answer."

"Not your business."

"Actually, it is my business when it's *your* hands down *my* pants."

A choked sound came from Finn's corner. Make that seven times, Soph thought to herself. Flipping a warning glare at Finn daring him to comment, she turned back to Zach and pushed back from the bench, her stiff wheeled stool scuffing slightly on the laminated floor.

"Fine. How do I tell my boss slash friend slash coworker slash ex-one-night-stand-turned-one-and-a-half-night-stand that I was horny, and angry, and filled with a bit of self loathing after a terrible failed Tinder pity date, all because I found out the night before that my boyfriend of five years, who dumped me a month and a half ago now, announced on Instagram that he is engaged to a girl I've never seen before in my life?"

They both ignored the sound of Finn choking yet again.

"Damn, Sunflower." Zach whistled long and low. "What did you do in your past life?"

"I'm a scientist. I don't believe in past lives." Sophia pulled off her lab goggles and rubbed at an imaginary smudge on the lens.

"Neither do I, but your life is making me this much closer to believing." Pushing off from the bench, Zach moved closer and snagged the stool next to her, straddling it in a way that made her stomach clench.

"In all seriousness, though," his voice dropped, and Sophia couldn't meet his gaze as his eyes turned tender. "Are you ok?"

~74~

Nodding jerkily, Sophia stood up, making her way to the exit where she could hang up her lab coat.

"Sophia." She paused at the sharpness in Zach's tone. "You know you can always take some time off work if you need it, right?"

"No!" She blurted quickly. "No. Being busy... it helps me not think about it. And I really don't want to think about — or talk about — it right now."

"I get it. I won't ask again unless you bring it up."

Sophia shakily breathed out in relief, placing her coat on her labelled peg. With Nef hanging out with Xander more and more, it was nice to have someone to talk to again. To check in on her. Sure, the whole 'just friends' thing was a work in progress at the moment, but good things took time.

Besides, Soph was self aware enough to know that in the aftermath of her heartbreak, she was feeling lonely. It was eating away at her, leaving hollow holes that ached to be filled with light conversation and laughter and the comfort of unconditional, ever-lasting love.

Unfortunately, she also knew that there was no scientific cure for this.

***

The next two months were a surprisingly pleasant blur.

In the first week after that uncomfortable conversation, consent forms from volunteer patients were signed and filed. Zach memorised her coffee order, so every morning she would show up at either her lab or his office to find a takeaway cup of a venti caramel mocha with oat milk and no whipped cream. He, of course, had a mug of plain black coffee with no sugar, like the monster he was.

In return, Soph did some reconnaissance and discovered that Zach had a weakness for blueberry muffins. Finn eventually started joining them for breakfast in the third week, contributing a different type of fruit each day.

By the second month, patients were booked in for the first round of randomisation and data collection. Sophia spent her week preparing various potential dosages of the drug Finn had created, and made more enemies out of the department's mice.

Her weekends were spent either with Nef, when she wasn't wedding planning with Xander, with Lilah and Zara, when they weren't busy with their own commitments, and slowly, with Zach. Brunches and library meet ups outside of work turned into regular dinners (occasionally joined by Bridget, Finn, and, rarely, Angelo), which then turned into karaoke or bowling or once, even, a coastal 'park run' that had Sophia swearing she would never let Zach talk her into exercise again.

She even enjoyed arguing with Zach over what drug would be a more ethical placebo for their clinical trial, until Finn stepped in, more passionate than she had ever seen him, almost hitting Zach in the face with his notebook as he gesticulated about the importance of monoclonal antibodies.

As the third month approached, her aching melancholy each night slowly dispersed into an appreciation for living alone, for the view outside her new apartment's window of wide roads and tree-lined streets, only ten minutes from Nef and twenty minutes from work. The heartbreak and loneliness were still there, but they were no longer at the front of her mind, which she was grateful for.

Halfway through the third month, Sophia was walking arm in arm with Zach and Finn, slightly tipsy and ready to belt out a terrible duet of One Direction's entire album for their weekly Saturday night hangouts when she got the email.

Detaching herself from her friends so she could check the notification, Sophia slowed to a stop on the pavement.

"Here we were, thinking you liked us." Finn cajoled from up ahead. He had slowly been spending more time without his notebook, and Soph hadn't decided yet whether she preferred the quiet version of him or the new, teasing version of him more. "We'll just wait here, don't worry."

Sticking her tongue out at him, Soph brushed a stray stand of hair back into her loose scarf. It was only October, but the weather was ridiculously cold already.

Taking a rallying breath, she opened the email as Zach doubled back towards her, leaving Finn to walk ahead.

"You ok, Sunflower?" He slung an arm over her shoulders, slowly pulling her towards the karaoke bar.

Nodding absently, she skimmed the email once, then twice. Out of the corner of her eye, she noticed Zach frowning at her, craning his neck to see her screen.

Sophia shoved her phone in her pocket and grinned at him. "I'm all good! Promise. I was just thinking about how fun it's going to be scoring higher than you when we sing 'Baby' tonight."

"Like you'll ever catch me singing to Justin Bieber," Zach snorted indignantly, moving to catch up with Finn.

"Oh, I know you will. I still have that video of you twerking to Backstreet Boys, remember?" Soph grinned sweetly, the email slowly drifting to the back of her mind. She'd tell Zach about it tomorrow, but tonight was for them.

"You really are going to hold that over me forever, aren't you."

He poked her in the ribs as they finally walked out of the cold and into the bar, Finn snagging their usual table and beelining to put his name down for every available Britney Spears song.

Soph poked him right back.

"Forever and always, Z. Get used to it."

CHAPTER 12

"Eliot E Tyler and Olivia A Johnson request the pleasure of your company to celebrate their marriage," Zach read out in a pompously exaggerated British accent.

"Sorry, but where is the pleasure in having your ex girlfriend at your wedding? You guys haven't even been broken up for six months." Finn was scowling at Sophia's phone, which Zach was currently holding in his hand.

"I am aware," Sophia grit out. Zach frowned in sympathy, and shot Finn a warning glance that he didn't see. Finding out your ex was cheating on you on Instagram was bad enough. Being invited to the fucking wedding would be like rubbing salt into a still bleeding wound.

"So? Do I accept or not?" A tinge of frustration had entered Soph's voice, but Zach knew it was directed at Eliot and not at them. Also likely at the insane workload that had built up over the weekend.

It was yet another Monday, and Zach was lounging in his office chair as their small gang crept through piles of past publications for their literature review. He reread the invitation, then glanced over to Soph again.

She looked stunning today, he thought. More than usual. The cold weather suited her, made her nose adorably red and gave her ears a cute pink tinge on the tips when she forgot to wear her beanie.

"Z," she flicked his knee sharply, then gestured for her phone back. "Yes or no?"

Zach blinked. "I vote yes, for the drama."

Finn cackled his agreement. "Remind me to never dump you then invite you to my wedding six months later."

"Fuck off, Finn," Zach and Soph said at the same time. Finn gave a gesture of surrender and turned back to his papers.

"I just feel like this was sent out of a feeling of guilt, or to rub it in my face. I can't tell, and I hate not knowing cause if I know then I can respond with an appropriate 'fuck you'," Sophia sighed and picked at the blueberry muffin in front of her.

"I think attending anyway is a great 'fuck you' for every potential reason you were invited," Finn drawled. "You should definitely go. And I'll happily be your plus one — I'll even bring my own popcorn."

Sophia smiled at that, relaxing back into her chair. Zach felt his stomach settle as he watched the tension leave her body, but thought better of reaching out to offer her a comforting touch. Something niggled at him though — he didn't like the idea of Finn being her plus one.

"Do you reckon this Olivia is pregnant?" Zach pondered around a mouthful of his own muffin.

Sophia and Finn turned to him at once, incredulous. Zach raised his eyebrows. Weren't they all thinking that?

"Why on Earth would you think that?" Finn asked, as Sophia said at the same time, "At thirty years old?"

Zach gave them both a pointed stare. "Thirty is far from a teenage pregnancy, Sunflower."

"I'm twenty one, thank you very much. I have been for eight years now." Sophia pouted, arms crossed.

He grinned at her. "I just meant that this is a pretty fast engagement period. Could be that one of their parents insisted they get hitched."

"Better her than me," Soph muttered with a shudder. "I'm not having kids till I get my PhD."

Zach could understand that. He had plenty of friends, nurses and doctors alike, who had said the same — career first, then family once they were certain they could financially support it. It was a smart idea, as long as it worked out.

Unfortunately, things didn't always go to plan, and he had seen just as many friends wait to finish residency then realise they were too old, or too single, to become parents.

Thoughts of little chubby cheeked kids with blonde curls and brown eyes filled his mind, grabbing at an imaginary older Sophia's hair with sticky fingers.

"When is the wedding, anyway?" Finn asked as he made more scribbles in his notebook. Zach shook his head, dispelling his thoughts. That was *way* too soon to be thinking about.

"End of February," Sophia huffed and turned back to her pile of papers. "But the engagement party is in two weeks."

Finn whistled and Zach frowned. It really was fast.

Comfortable silence filled the room along with the morning sunlight as the trio went back to working on their research, Zach trying to ignore more thoughts of kids and Sophia.

Zach savoured the next few minutes as he fell into a paper by an old mentor, highlighting sections of methodology that he thought could be replicated in their trial. This was a familiar pattern to him, the flow charting and abstract analysing and culling of what would and wouldn't be relevant. This was safe — more safe than dwelling on Sophia potentially going to her ex's wedding. His Sunflower wasn't fragile, but Zach would rather swallow nails than think about Sophia in the same room as the man who had hurt her so badly, so recently.

"I think I'll go to the engagement party, then see how that goes before RSVP-ing to the actual wedding." Sophia's warm voice cut in like she had read his mind and decided to torture him.

Swallowing his sigh, Zach reminded himself that he protected his friends, like he did his best to protect his patients. So he would swallow nails and think about this, because he had to make sure he could consider all potential outcomes so he could keep her as safe as possible. Physically and emotionally, whether she knew it or not.

Both their decisions now verbally and silently determined, the rest of their day went by buried in medical journals.

CHAPTER 13

An outpouring of swear words fell from Sophia's mouth as she tried and failed to zip up the back of her dress.

It was four in the afternoon on the day of Eliot and Olivia's engagement party, and so far the day was going better than anticipated. Naturally, that had been too good to last, so even though Sophia had finished work early and was now alone in the hospital changing rooms, she just couldn't get this stupid. Dress. To. Zip!

Leaning a hip against a locker door, Sophia reached both hands behind her to try gain more leverage on the stubborn fabric. Face twisting as she pulled harder, she contemplated just letting the material rip and not going to the party at all.

But it really was a gorgeous dress, and like any self-respecting woman going to her ex's engagement party and meeting the woman he had cheated on her with for god knows how long for the first time, it would be a waste if she couldn't show it off a bit.

Nef's voice floated through her head, gleefully calling her a petty bitch.

You know what? In this case, justified. Sophia would be a petty bitch through and through — a polite one, though, because god forbid she made a scene this evening. She may still be a heartbroken, seething mess deep down, but she would *not* let Eliot see that he got to her.

The zipper finally gave, and the glittery metallic gold fabric moulded to her body. Despite the skin-tight fit, it was beautifully modest: a small v-neck at the front with a deeper, matching v at the back, cinching her waist naturally before falling over her thighs to mid-calf. A thin slit on the left crept up her thigh, giving a glimpse of flesh that she had shaved and polished to perfection the previous night.

Final touches included touching up her subtle nude makeup, putting her blonde hair up in an elegant twist (it had finally grown long enough), adding black crystal earrings, and lastly, matching sky-high black stilettos.

With one last glare in the mirror, Sophia acknowledged that it was finally time to go. She fit the theme (gold, how original), was dressed modestly enough to not insult the bride-to-be, and felt confident (ish) that she wouldn't do anything embarrassing when she saw her ex.

Grabbing her small black purse, Soph sped out of the change rooms and powered into the main hall of the wards. She had almost made it halfway to the exit when a tall, gorgeous figure caught her eye.

A group of men in suits were walking out of one of the small presentation rooms. It must have been some kind of medical conference or case study, because some had stethoscopes around their neck while others wore their white coats. But what had caught her eye — or rather, who — was Zach.

Over the last few months, Soph had thought that she had grown used to his sheer magnetism and attractiveness. But as he sauntered out, dimple and grin on full display, baby blue shirt sleeves rolled up to show off his muscular, tan forearms, Soph realised that she was mistaken.

He glanced up from his colleagues mid-laughter, and his gaze caught on hers.

Time slowed down, and Sophia felt an odd sensation, like she was falling into his eyes.

Bam!

In this case, she was simply falling, having stepped just slightly incorrectly in her heels.

Sophia cried out as her left knee slammed into the laminated floor. In a heartbeat, a concerned Zach was kneeling in front of her, tilting her chin up towards him.

"I'm fine!" Sophia squeaked out. "Z, please."

Zach didn't speak, just kept tilting her chin from side to side, inspecting her face intensely before releasing her and moving to her knee. Sprawled out on her butt, Soph just watched as he hovered his hands over her injured leg.

"Can I check your leg?" Zach rumbled as he held her gaze.

Nodding silently, she held her breath as Zach reached to pull up her skirts. Hesitating, he looked around as if just now noticing they had drawn a small gathering of worried staff and patients. Frowning, Zach turned back to her.

"I'm going to carry you to a private room, Soph." His tone brooked no argument, but even if she had wanted to protest she wasn't given time.

With surprising ease, Zach swept Sophia up into his arms, one arm under her knees and the other around her back. With no other choice to help balance herself, Soph flung her arms around his neck, and tried her best to avoid the stares of everyone around them as Zach briskly walked them to the nearest empty patient room.

She must have been redder than a beetroot by the time Zach gently placed her on a bed and drew the blue curtains closed around them for further privacy.

"Z, really, I'm fine. And I really need to get going…" She trailed off as she saw his face. He was her friend, but this was the face of the doctor — Dr Zach Hayes, the attending.

The gaunt expression she had never seen on him before drew on her heartstrings.

"Please, Sunflower," Zach's voice somehow dropped even lower. "Let me check your leg. For me."

How could she say no to him?

Nodding again, she leant back against the hospital bed, careful not to ruin her hair.

With careful, practiced movements, Zach washed his hands with medical-grade sanitiser before stepping over to her right side.

"I'm going to touch and move your knee, Sophia, and I need you to let me know if you feel any pain at any point in time."

The order in his voice left no room for argument. Zach slowly drew the hem of her dress up her thigh, until the split fell over her leg to expose her sore knee. Already, a brilliant purple-blue hue was spread across the top and side of it from her fall, but Sophia was watching Zach's face, the way his eyes roved down her neck, her waist, her legs.

"If you want me to stop, just say so," he warned.

All of a sudden, his hands were on her leg, both thumbs firmly sliding up the front of her shin to the base of her knee. Sophia gasped at his warm touch, the rough slide of his skin against hers.

"Does this hurt?" Zach paused his movements, face to face with her.

"No," Soph swallowed hard. It felt nice, but she wasn't about to say that.

Gently, Zach rubbed his thumbs around the side of her knee, cupping the back of it and pressing down. She could have sworn his thumb made a slight stroking movement. Or maybe that was just part of the exam?

"I'm just making sure there's no fracture," Zach murmured, hands still wrapped securely around her knee.

Sophia's breaths sped up as he moved her dress higher, smoothing a rough palm down her thigh to her knee and doing some sort of swiping movement.

"No effusion..." Zach's teeth seemed clenched in concentration, highlighting his strong jawline and the hint of freshly shaved stubble.

Zach repeated the swiping movement, and every touch of his hand on her upper and inner thigh, the back of her knee, made her feel hot and cold at the same time, a pool of warmth gathering at her centre.

Suddenly, Zach was even closer. He had manoeuvred onto the bed, and his thigh was somehow wedged under hers. His very firm, taut, thigh.

He must have sensed her confusion, because he paused again to explain that he was going to pull on her leg somehow, something about ligaments, but all she could focus on was his heat and the smell of his cologne

— something spicy she couldn't place — and the way he was now contorting her leg into different positions.

The way he moved her knee to her chest had her core contracting, remembering a similar position all those months ago. When he dragged her knee back to a flat position, she grit her teeth to prevent a whimper as Zach withdrew his touch slowly, hands sliding down her bare skin to her ankle.

Finally, he had her stand and hold onto his arms for balance, made her do some twisty dance movement that would somehow tell him about her stability. Barefoot, she barely reached his chin. Sophia tried craning her face to meet his gaze, but Zach was firmly stuck in doctor mode - eyes ahead, jaw tight, grip on her firm, stable, but clinical.

It was a good thing, Soph reminded herself. They were just friends. They didn't touch like this, and they wouldn't breach the boundary they had mutually established. A small part of her, however, admitted its disappointment that Zach didn't seem to be as affected by her touch as she clearly was by his.

It took longer than she would have liked to get herself to release his arms. Stepping back, Sophia tried to mask her jagged breathing. Zach turned away to use the sanitiser again, a bubble of awkward silence filling the room.

"How am I, doctor?" Sophia hated the slight breathlessness in her voice.

Spinning around, eyes flaring, Zach cleared his throat once, then twice. "You're perfect. I mean, your knee is perfect. Totally normal and healthy. Just a bruise."

His chest was heaving almost as fast as her own. Slipping her heels back on, Sophia edged towards the blue curtains, ready to leave.

"Thanks for doing that, Zach, You didn't have to."

"I know. But I always will."

He followed her out of the room and back into the hallway, easily keeping pace with her long strides.

"You sure you'll be ok going to the engagement party tonight?" Zach asked.

"It'll be easy peasy lemon squeezy," Sophia determinedly charged towards the exit, pulling out her phone to call a cab. Her stomach was still a warm mess of *something* when she looked at her friend, flashes of his capable hands on her thighs spinning behind her eyes on repeat.

One exam, one innocent check up, and she felt like a rug had been pulled out from under her.

"You're not calling a cab, are you?" Zach was still trailing her, pulling his shirt sleeves down and re-buttoning them.

"Of course I am. Do I look like I have a car let alone a licence?" She sped up, feeling the passing of time like an anchor. She was so late. What would Eliot say?

Stopping at the curb, Soph checked her phone for the cab again, ignoring the timestamp taunting her at the top of her screen.

Walking up next to her in his impeccable suit, Zach peeked over her shoulder, far too close for comfort. Then, with an annoyingly charming arrogance that she was starting to get used to, he plucked her phone out of her hands and cancelled the cab she had ordered.

"Z, what the fuck?" Sophia gaped.

But Zach had already grabbed her hand and started leading her towards the car park out the front.

"It's going to get dark soon, you have an injured knee, and you're about to go to your ex's engagement party. I'm driving."

Five minutes later, when Sophia was buckled in the passenger seat of Zach's subtly fancy car and they were cruising towards the event hall, surrounded by the delicious scent of his cologne, she let herself relax marginally.

Having Zach by her side tonight was far from planned. But god did it make just the thought of the next few hours feel a little less heavy.

CHAPTER 14

Fortunately driving required all his concentration, because otherwise Zach's head would be more of a mess than usual. Every red light was a curse, however, as it gave him time to think about his recklessness. First examining Sophia, then offering to drive her to the party. And while he might try to deny it, he knew beyond a single doubt that the second he parked, he would be walking in with her.

Just in case she tripped again. That was the only reason.

His hands flexed on the wheel, the phantom feeling of Sophia's smooth skin under his palm making his heart race. He ignored it.

Shooting Sophia a look out of the corner of his eye, Zach noted how the tension in her shoulders from earlier seemed to be easing as she watched the road race past her window.

He may be a reckless, hormone driven man tonight, but at least he knew he was giving his friend some measure of comfort.

They pulled up to the address Sophia had given him in silence, a slight breeze outside the car rustling the branches of the tall maple trees lining the side of the street. The venue itself was a sandstone and marble hotel with a large ballroom, and Zach vaguely remembered being to some conferences here before.

Speaking of conferences, it was a good thing he had worn a suit for his today. But clothing would be the last thing stopping him from providing support to a friend who needed it.

A light touch on his lower thigh had his stomach muscles clenching.

"Z..." Sophia was barely meeting his eyes, her own a mesmerising blue shadowed by thick black-coated lashes.

"Of course I'll come in with you." Zach answered her unspoken question without hesitation, covering her hand with his own.

He swore that her grateful smile could have cured cancer.

Tearing himself away with effort, Zach rushed around the car to open the door for Soph. With an exaggerated flourish, she accepted his arm and they started up the concrete path to the brightly lit revolving doors.

Straight into the snake's lair.

***

"At least it's an open bar," Sophia grumbled as she drained half of her second cocktail through a pink straw, her pouty lips wrapped around the cardboard in a dangerously distracting way.

Trying to think about anything other than the memory of what those lips could do — *have* done — to him, Zach threw back his own negroni to match her.

"At least I'm not on call tonight," he nodded at the bartender for two more drinks, content to stay at their perch on a pair of stools at the side of the room for the rest of the night.

The ballroom had been properly decked out. White balloons, gold balloons, and clear balloons with gold sparkles flanked the entrance and formed an arch over a table full of finger food. Glittery gold candles were placed around the room, and dim lighting warmed the faces of various gold-plated guests as they swayed uncoordinatedly to a live string quartet.

"I'm already a bitch for being here, so I'm just gonna come out and say it. Reckon he's marrying her for the money?" Sophia plucked her maraschino cherry between her manicured nails and chewed it slowly, face unreadable. This was a pretty lavish engagement party for a six month public courtship.

Zach snorted. "I thought we established its because of the baby."

A smile cracked her face, straight through his heart as he saw the flash of pain in her eyes. Being here hurt her. She hid it well, but Zach saw right through it.

Tell me what to do, he almost begged her. *Tell me how I can ease your pain.*

But he stayed silent, instead watching as gauzy cloud of white approached them, topped with a head of long brown hair and ending with tanned, willowy legs.

"Do you think that's the fiancé?" Sophia whispered sarcastically out of the corner of her mouth, hands around a third drink — a bright, health-concerning blue this time.

Zach held his tongue as the woman drew up to their seats, a polite but unfamiliar smile on her face. She was pretty, in an average kind of way Zach thought. High cheekbones, full mouth, brown eyes, and glowing with the happiness of a bride-to-be. She was lovely, and she obviously looked great in her photos next to Eliot, but she just wasn't… sunflower pretty, if that made sense.

It made sense to him, especially as he glanced between the fiancé and Sophia.

"Hi!" The woman held out a hand, long nails painted a metallic gold and matching the champagne glass she was holding. "I'm Olivia, but you guys can call me Liv. I don't think we've met yet, are you guys friends of Eliot's?"

Sensing Sophia's discomfort, Zach responded for her. "She is, I'm just a plus one. Congratulations on your engagement."

Olivia — Liv — beamed at him. "Thank you! And thank you for coming! If you guys are friends of Eliot's I'll have to drag him over, he's been flitting around all night."

Her peal of laughter drowned out Sophia's polite protest, and Liv scanned the room for her future groom. Spotting him in the middle of the dance floor with a group of guys also dressed in suits, she waved him over determinedly.

Without thinking, Zach grabbed Sophia's hand as her ex approached, not even flinching when she squeezed hard enough to cut off his circulation.

Without yet looking at them, Eliot swung his fiancé into a dip, plopping a long, open mouthed, unwarranted kiss onto her lips.

Sophia squeezed his hand even harder. He didn't blame her. And he didn't examine the flash of discomfort in the pit of his stomach when he clocked how Sophia was looking at Eliot.

The couple finally disengaged, whispering sweet nothings in each other's ears before turning to him and Sophia. With no small amount of pleasure, Zach watched Eliot's face pale slightly beneath his gold-embroidered white suit as he recognised Sophia.

"Hey!" Eliot's voice was deeper than Zach had expected. Not as deep as his own, though. The man crossed his arms awkwardly, and Zach noted the way his muscles bunched. Still not as much as his own did.

Jesus Christ, was he really getting into an imaginary pissing competition with his friend's ex? At said ex's engagement party to another woman? What was wrong with him?

"Hey, Eliot!" Sophia's smile was sweeter and more artificial than xylitol. "Congratulations on your engagement. Love the ring you picked out."

A slight flush coloured Eliot's cheeks, and Zach bit his own to stop his smirk. As much as he wanted Sophia to get her well-deserved revenge, he wasn't going to let her crash and burn publicly.

"Thanks for inviting us. It's a great party," Zach added a bit too quickly.

"Ellie, I was just introducing myself to your friends. I've never met them before!" Liv swayed slightly, clearly a little tipsy.

Catching her subtly, Eliot murmured an agreement. "Liv, this is my... old friend, Sophia. We went to high school together."

"Wow, it must be nice to have such old friends. It's so special that you can be here today," she smiled at Liv, and Zach was surprised when Sophia smiled back.

"It is special," Sophia agreed. "We even went to college together! Ellie and I have known each other a long time."

Zach barely noticed the emphasis she put on the man's nickname, the vitriol was that subtle. Picking up on Sophia's rising animosity, he decided that it was time to spare all parties from further interaction.

"Unfortunately, we can't stay long tonight. But we wanted to drop by and give our well-wishes in person."

"Leaving so soon?" Liv looked genuinely disappointed. Eliot, however, deflated with relief and ran a hand through his sandy hair, coifed with far too much gel.

"Coming late and leaving early," Eliot said with a laugh. "Thanks for making the effort."

Sophia frowned and Zach put a comforting hand on her shoulder.

"Sorry we couldn't stay longer. I have an early work shift tomorrow, and Sophia injured herself on the way over so we had to take care of that first. We really appreciate you understanding, but hopefully we'll see you both again soon!" Zach forced a grin and turned Sophia towards the exit, ready to make a quick escape. God, the way this night had turned.

"Stay a bit longer! What do you do for work?"

Liv took that moment to flit away with a squeal towards a gaggle of girls on the other side of the room.

"I'm a doctor." Zach's voice was clipped.

Sophia still had a death grip on his hand, and was clearly itching to leave. He would never say that coming here had been a bad idea, but staying longer definitely would be.

"What kind of doctor?" Eliot clapped Zach on the back, eyes darting to where his hand was locked around Soph's.

"Medical oncology." He gritted. "We really do have to leave, I need to check Soph's leg again."

"Her leg?" A furrow appeared between Eliot's brow. "What happened?"

Considering that this guy had the sheer chutzpah to invite his ex to his engagement party within five months of ending their relationship, Zach wasn't surprised it had taken this long for Sophia's injury to register for him.

"Just a slip! Nothing to worry about." Sophia interjected with a thin lipped smile, finally easing up on her grip on his hand. "Come on, Z, let's go."

"Z?" Eliot repeated. The theme tonight seemed to be confusion rather than gold.

"My nickname. I'm Zach, by the way, and I already know you're Eliot."

Stay calm, stay calm, stay calm.

Usually his patience was way better than this, especially considering the innumerable difficult patients he'd dealt with for years, but seeing Sophia's slipping seemed to ruin him.

Taking a step away again, Zach was ready to throw Soph over his shoulder and make a run for it. There was no way he would let her stay in this nightmare any longer.

"Are you two together?"

Eliot's statement hung in the air like a noxious cloud. Zach's eyes bounced between Eliot, Sophia, and the door. How was he supposed to answer that?

With a clear 'no', you idiot, he thought to himself. You both have made it clear you're just friends. Saying yes out of spite would be foolish beyond belief.

"Sorry," Eliot sounded anything but. "I just didn't realise doctors looked after their patients this well."

"We're just friends —" Zach started at the same time Sophia said "Fine, we're dating. And we need to go."

Punctuating her statement with a firm but chaste kiss on Zach's mouth, Sophia stormed towards the exit at last, half of her remaining lipstick on his lower lip and chin.

Tugged along like the tide with Sophia as his moon, Zach was surprised by how steadily his legs carried him outside the hotel and back to his car.

What had they just done?

CHAPTER 15

Having deep conversations over a stiff drink was becoming a habit.

Drumming her nails on the rim of her piña colada, Sophia took a long sip through her straw as she pretended to look everywhere except at Zach. Her lipstick was still smudged on his mouth, and she had to shove down the weird feeling it set off in her chest. Surely it's just the three cocktails she'd downed this evening, more standards than she usually would have.

"So..." Zach chugged another beer back, before grimacing. "I almost wish we were still at the open bar."

"You're an attending doctor. You can afford better beer if you want."

Zach shrugged. "So. Alcohol and discussions about kissing each other. If I didn't know any better, I'd say you wanted to forget our 'just friends' agreement."

Sophia winced in apology. "I wasn't thinking."

"I'm not mad, Soph," Zach leant forward. "Eliot was driving me mad too. I don't know how you were with him for so long."

His statement clanged through her, a repetitive loop echoing what she thought every night before sleep. If tonight had proved anything, it was that she had avoided a really massive red flag. Even if she still ached from how badly said red flag had hurt her.

Mistaking his earlier statement for her sudden mood change, Zach winced. "Sorry Soph, that was a poor joke. I'll always respect your wishes, and we won't go beyond just friends."

She nodded vaguely, but her mind started ticking. She couldn't deny that the kiss had been a bit selfish of her. And maybe if she hadn't gone tonight, she would have been a bit more ready to move on — with whoever. She wasn't specifically thinking about Zach.

But seeing Olivia wearing what should have been her ring, even though Eliot had never actually given it to her, had twisted the knife in deep.

The worst part? Sophia actually *liked* Olivia. She had been sweet, and genuine, and polite, despite most likely knowing exactly what kind of 'old friend' Sophia was to

Eliot. And at the end of the day, what Eliot had done wasn't Liv's fault. Maybe she didn't even know about the ring.

But that itching, restless feeling that had sat on her chest choking her all night... she couldn't stand to be pitied. The poor jilted ex who was now showing up at the nuptials, alone. Pathetic: everyone must be thinking it.

The only thing that had let her breath was Zach's hand in hers, anchoring her to reality.

"What if..." Soph bit her lip. It was a stupid idea. One only in crazy rom-coms that usually ended badly.

Zach raised an eyebrow. "You know I love a good edging, Sunflower, but I can see those cogs spinning. What're you thinking?"

Her face must be so red right now. The last thing she needed was to be reminded of Zach's bedroom preferences. Preferences that aligned with her needs perfectly...

Shaking her head, Sophia looked Zach directly in the eyes.

"I have a crazy, stupid, idea. But there are going to be ground rules."

"I'm a doctor," Zach gave a lazy smile laced with arrogance. "Rules are my middle name."

Rolling her eyes, Sophia reached for a spare chip at the bottom of the bowl to the side of them, before flicking at him with a tiny smile.

"What if we actually fake dated?"

Zach swore the happily engaged couple must have laced the bar with something, because tonight had not gone anything like he had expected.

"Dated," he repeated faintly, running a hand over his stubble. "You and me, dating?"

"*Fake* dating," Sophia corrected. She looked dead serious. "Just until the wedding is over, and only while we're at any wedding-related events."

"Yeah, cause *that's* going to go well. Remember the last time we were closer to dating than friends?" Zach scoffed.

His heart was racing under his shirt, but he refused to show any signs of being affected. What would fake dating entail?

Please, god, he prayed silently, let it include me getting to taste those sweet lips again.

Sophia was fidgeting with a napkin, folding it in half then half again before shredding it into small pieces. She was so cute when she was flustered. She should not be this cute when she was suggesting they fake dated.

"We make ground rules, obviously. When we're not around others, or when we're just out with friends — who we'll tell what's going on — we keep to our established friends-only boundaries.

But when we're at any of the wedding events, like the rehearsal dinner and ceremony and reception, we act like a couple."

Zach's brain short circuited as he imagined all the couple-y things he wanted to do to his best friend.

"Why?" He managed to grind out.

Sophia raised an eyebrow, and damn if her looking all prim and proper and in control didn't do things to his aching dick.

Get it together, man. One chaste peck out of... spite? Did not a relationship make.

"Why fake date? I mean I get that it's awkward now to say that we 'broke up', but you could just go alone and say I was busy in theatre. You don't need me."

"I don't need you," Sophia agreed too readily for Zach's liking. "But I want you."

Her voice turned softer as stars danced in front of Zach's eyes at her statement.

"You're my best friend, Z. I mean, in addition to Nef, but she's more my sister so... you get it. I honestly don't think I could have gotten through tonight without you, and I don't want to go to the rest of the wedding shit without you."

"You know I'd go with you in a heartbeat, right? Fake dating or not?" Sophia seemed taken aback by the passion in his voice, but she nodded.

Good. It was vital to him that she knew how completely he was on her side.

"Whatever you need, Sunflower. I'm yours." Leaning forward, Zach brushed a loose strand of hair behind her ear, where it had slipped free of her bun.

He might have let his thumb linger on the apple of her cheek a beat longer than necessary. And Sophia might have shifted as though she was going to turn her head into his palm, but that could just be his hopeful imagination.

"Also, I have to ask: we could have just left. You didn't need to say we were dating. As much as I'm in for the drama, I don't… I don't want to be some tool for you to use to get back at Eliot." The words tasted bitter on his tongue, but Zach had to make sure he wasn't going to help her with some grand ploy to win back this Zack Snyder loving man-baby.

"Eliot is the last person I would do anything for," Sophia practically snarled. "I just… I want to go to the wedding and everything to satisfy my own morbid curiosity. And I want everyone to see that I'm still… desirable, I guess. Wanted. And I don't want to… I *can't* go alone. Plus, I would look ten kinds of foolish if I showed up without you at the rehearsal dinner and said we'd broken up or that I'd lied about us dating."

"Well, we can't have someone as damn intelligent as you looking foolish, can we."

Sophia's eyes snapped to his, and a warm smile bloomed over her face as she realised he meant it.

"So you're in?"

"I'm in."

I'm always in when it comes to you. But Zach didn't let that thought turn into words.

Slowly, the pair gathered their things and headed out of the bar and back into the cold streets. Sophia brushed past him as Zach held the door open, and he couldn't resist throwing out one last cliche.

"Just make sure you don't fall in love with me by the end of this," he winked.

Sophia huffed a laugh as she pulled on her beanie, covering her stunning blonde waves.

"Not a problem, Z," Soph smirked.

If Zach said it enough, though, maybe he could jinx them.

CHAPTER 16

"Fake dating," Zach's sister propped her chin on a perfectly manicured hand and stared into his soul like she wasn't three years younger than him.

"Yes, Mira, you've said it five times now." Pinching the bridge of his nose, Zach settled back into the plush couch at Mira's apartment.

It was small and cozy, reminiscent of how she used to decorate her childhood bedroom, the walls covered in scattered polaroids of her friends and framed photos of the two of them with their parents. Even though both of them had moved out of home years ago now, their own places were as much each other's homes as before.

Mira's tough love also still felt like home.

"I knew you were stupid, but this is a new low, Z. Your new best friend, who you've already had a one night stand with — and again, please do *not* tell me the details — who you're also working with. The fuck is wrong with you?"

Grumbling, Zach made a rude gesture, which Mira easily returned from her place across from him.

"I wasn't thinking," Zach mumbled. Well, he was thinking — about how good it felt having Soph's lips on his again, even for just a split second.

"Duh," Mira smirked. They shared the same mouth, the same eyes, the same hair colour, though Mira's was in a permanent state of unruliness.

"What was I supposed to do, Ra-Ra? Leave her to go alone next time?" He intentionally used her childhood nickname, which he knew would raise her hackles. Serves her right for calling him stupid.

"Yes!" Mira threw up her hands. "Look, from what you've told me, she's highly intelligent and capable, and doesn't need you. You're obviously head over heels for her already, and this is going to complicate things. You should back out of it now before it's too late."

"I'm not backing out. And I'm not head over heels for her." Zach sounded unconvincing even to himself.

"Sure." Sarcasm practically dripped from his sister. "You just agreed to be your best friend's fake date to her ex's wedding out of the pure goodness of your heart."

Zach drew a hand over his stubble, the roughness of it soothing him while also reminding him that he needed to shave soon.

"It was unplanned, and it's only for when we're at the events. It's not going to complicate work, and it's not going to mean anything. I told you already, it was a spur of the moment spite fuelled kiss —"

"And then you short circuited because you're," Mira made a crude whipping sound, and Zach winced/ grinned at her antics.

Just then, his phone chimed. Reading the message, he couldn't stop his grin from spreading.

HEY LOVER, IF I'M BEING SUBJECTED TO THE TORTURE OF A REHEARSAL DINNER YOU SURE AS HELL ARE TOO. I'VE RSVP'D US. DON'T YOU DARE HAVE A NIGHT SHIFT.

Attached was a photo of the invitation, set for a late evening end of January, with the wedding itself the next day. So really, that was only two consecutive events where they would be dating. *Fake* dating.

"Ten bucks that's Sophia," Mira deadpanned.

"Mom doesn't let us bet anymore."

"Don't tell Mom then."

Sighing, Zach used his spare hand to fish out a ten dollar note from his wallet and forked it over.

"See?" Mira smiled jubilantly. "Whipped for your fake date."

❖

Sophia was pretty sure the flush on her cheeks hadn't disappeared in the week since Zach told her not to fall in love with him.

His deep, rough voice, so at odds with his gentle bedside manner, played on repeat through her mind as she replayed their conversation for the millionth time.

It was nearly two in the morning, and while it was a Friday night (meaning she could sleep in as much as she needed tomorrow), Sophia had never felt more on edge.

The kiss. Fake dating. Zach's warm, soft palm on her cheek. The smell of his cologne lingering on her dress after the party.

Her skin felt too tight, and despite the window she had thrown open, the cool breeze wasn't doing anything to ease the tingling heat that had taken up permanent residence in her stomach since that night.

What on earth was wrong with her? She had never felt like this before.

A small voice in the back of her mind whispered that she was lying to herself. She knew exactly when she had last felt like this, and it was in the delicate months before she had started dating Eliot. Had it really been so long since she'd felt real, toe curling, panty-melting desire, that she had forgotten what it felt like?

Rolling over in bed, Sophia pressed a hand to her cheeks as though she could will the redness away.

She must be an idiot, if she thought the fake dating idea would end in anything other than disaster. Why had she kissed him? What possessed her to get them both into this messy charade? Was she really so childish and petty that she would fake date her best friend/boss to spite her ex?

Questions rolled in her mind, alternating between the feeling of Zach's soft lips under hers.

Stupid, stupid, stupid.

Except...

Well, we can't have someone as damn intelligent as you looking foolish, can we?

Zach's voice drifted to the front of her mind again. He had meant it, too. He really thought she was intelligent.

For some reason, that touched a nerve Sophia hadn't realised was raw. The more she spent time with Zach, the more she realised what a good person he was. The more she thought about what it would have been like if they had met under different circumstances, or a different time — not the night of her break up.

Tonight, especially, she mostly thought about what that night had been like.

Sophia remembered the morning after, the ache between her legs and the bite mark she had found later on the bottom swell of her breast. The hickey on her upper inner thigh.

Wetness pooled between her thighs as the clock ticked towards morning. She could not, would not, entertain fantasies about Zach.

Could she?

Sophia pretended she wasn't willing her hand to move as it snuck down the front of her matching pyjama set. The smooth cotton of her shirt was a teasing weight against her nipples, which had pebbled into sensitive rocks. Wedging the soft material of her shorts to the side, she slipped a finger through her folds, gathering the wetness onto her middle finger before dragging it ever-so-gently around her clit.

Zach had probably used his tongue just like this. If he did it again, would he lick in just the way she liked? Sophia drew her finger in smaller, higher circles, hips involuntarily shifting beneath her aqua sheets.

He probably would, she decided. He would lick her nice and slow, before sucking on her clit with just enough pressure to make her back bow. He would flick it with his tongue, before slipping two fingers inside her tight centre like she was doing now, pumping until he hit the spot that would make her see stars.

Panting, Sophia kept working her fingers deeper, shirt riding up her chest as she imagined Zach below her this time: hair ruffled, chest bare with a sprinkling of hair, beard scratchy against her inner thighs in the best way as she rode his tongue until she orgasmed. She wouldn't let up, wouldn't let him stop until he had licked her clean, and then she would finally give him his reward as she —

A whimper that sounded suspiciously like Zach's name spilled from her lips as Sophia tipped over the edge, pleasure running up her spine as she collapsed onto her side.

Before Sophia had a chance to regret what she had just done, she was asleep.

CHAPTER 17

November turned into December, and before Sophia knew it she had looked up from the piles of data she had obtained (from both mice and human subjects) and the hospital Christmas party was around the corner.

Finn, Zach, and herself had already made plans to go for drinks beforehand, and Finn had given them each an atrociously ugly Christmas sweater to wear for the night — along with promises that whoever took theirs off first was in charge of buying the first round.

Fortunately, the fake dating agreement seemed to have only made her and Zach closer. They shared a secret now, accompanied by secret smiles and knowing glances, inside jokes that they didn't even have to speak aloud to know it had been told.

And Sophia had been so tired each night after analysing the effects of their new drug on her test subjects that she hadn't even thought about repeating those fantasies she'd entertained all those weeks ago.

Instead, her dreams were filled with images of test tubes and syringes; what made other's dreams into nightmares only helped her wake each day determined to do her best so their paper would get published, would have tangible results for patients.

From the look of the documents she had open on her laptop in front of her, Sophia knew that they really were on to something.

"Look," she murmured softly as she pointed at one of the de-identified lines of data on the spreadsheet.

Zach leant over her shoulder to squint at the screen.

"That's statistically significant!" He breathed excitedly. "Are they all like this?"

"The only data we need to discount is Mrs Reading, but she'll make a great discussion point about adherence and comorbidities." Sophia grinned.

The drug — a new type of monoclonal antibody that was some unpronounceable word ending in 'mab' — was showing clear signs of extending life expectancy for patients with advanced bowel cancer, even if just by two months. Miraculously (though this could be the placebo affect), some patients were even claiming that it helped lessen their associated pain.

Zach spun away from her laptop and did a shockingly awful combination of dance moves that must have been popular in the eighties.

"This is incredible! We still have at least nine months to go, who knows what we can do with this! If I write up the methodology next week, do you want to meet up to do edits and then the results? I'll get Finn on the statistics and drug models for the appendix, and then..."

Sophia stopped hearing Zach when he whipped out a pair of round-framed wire glasses and shoved them onto his face, circling back to her side to peer at the data again.

Jesus mother-fucking Christ and the name of all things holy.

She knew Zach was hot. But Zach with glasses was a whole different level of hot. He was *Hot*, hot. Sexy. Edible. All with capital letters.

Taking a sip from her water bottle to combat her suddenly dry mouth, Sophia tried to nonchalantly join the conversation again.

"...trial with different types of opioids to see whether the pain is impacted. What do you think, Sunflower?"

Soph felt her cheeks heat at the nickname. She would never live it down if he discovered she had even impulse bought a set of sunflower pyjamas from Peter Alexander the other day because it reminded her of him.

"I think that sounds great," Sophia tried to concentrate on Zach's words, but that just made her glance at his lips.

"I need to go to the bathroom," she blurted. Not looking Zach in the eye, she rushed out of his office and down the hall to the ladies rooms, where she promptly sequestered herself in a bathroom stall.

What was *wrong* with her? Those fantasies last month... she had done her best to put that whole thing behind her. With the rehearsal dinner not for another few weeks, she didn't have to think about the fake dating situation. So why did Zach have to go ruin her composure just because he put on *glasses*?

Pulling out her phone, she went to her group chat with the girls. They had all been informed about the situation, but what was she planning to tell them now? That she was crushing and fantasising about her best friend and boss in ways that would give HR a heart attack?

Leaning against the stall door, Soph gave herself a short pep talk, knowing that she'd have to go back to the office and see Zach again soon.

She was a big girl. She could do this.

She would not crush on her fake date, especially when she hadn't yet been single for a year.

And wasn't that the crux of it? Zach being her best friend, her boss, that could all be overcome with some discussions with HR and some hard ground rules and good communication. Soph knew it would probably be the best relationship she'd ever have.

But just thinking that still felt like a betrayal to Eliot, despite the fact that he had either been seeing someone throughout their relationship or straight after, and was now marrying this woman.

Following this budding crush would get her and Zach nowhere. It wouldn't be fair to either of them.

But it wouldn't hurt to just… think about it? Right?

That, Sophia could do. Taking a deep breath, Sophia left the bathrooms and headed back to the office.

Thinking about Zach was acceptable. But she would never act on it. Not until she was well and truly over Eliot.

Aside from that weird moment in his office two weeks ago, Sophia seemed to be acting pretty normally. Not that Zach had been paying close enough attention to know what her normal and abnormal behaviour was. Cause that would be a bit creepy, and might indicate he had a crush. Which as a thirty one year old, he most certainly did not.

"I do not have crushes," he muttered under his breath.

"What was that?" Of course Finn heard him, despite being deep in his notebook as usual.

"I just said that your sweaters are really ugly," Zach smirked.

"I kind of love mine, actually," Sophia sat at the table opposite him at the bar. "But by all means, if you don't like yours, take it off."

Zach flushed at his self-interpreted innuendo, trying to pass it off as indignation.

"In your dreams, Sunflower. It'll be a dark day in hell when I buy people rounds."

It was a dark day in hell when Zach had to put on the monstrosity of wool in the first place. It was a garish orange that tried to pass for red, with vomit-green reindeer crocheted in patterns. He knew it was supposed to look like they were dancing, but to him it just looked like animal cruelty.

"I would bet good money that I could have you buying me a drink in minutes regardless of the sweaters."

Zach dragged his gaze slowly over Sophia, taking in the proud tilt of her lips and the way her eyes seemed to sparkle in the warm lighting. Even in that horrid outfit, she was gorgeous, a living, breathing fantasy of what it could be like if fake dating turned to real dating...

"I'm sure you could, Sunflower. But that's not the bet."

A sense of primal satisfaction filled his chest as a blush spread over Sophia's cheeks. He wanted to lean forward and lick the colour like syrup.

Finn saved him before his stare could turn into plain eye-fucking.

"We're about to be fashionably late for the party. Shall we go before Bridget drinks enough to change the playlist to K-Pop covers of 'All I Want For Christmas Is You'?"

"Would she really do that?" Sophia looked delightedly incredulous.

"Would and has," Zach laughed. "In her defence, they are pretty catchy."

They argued the merits of K-Pop covers for the rest of the walk back to the hospital, Sophia wedged between himself and Finn, her perfume making Zach feel slightly heady, her gloved hand brushing his with every second step.

Just friends. No crushes. Fake dating.

He had told her to be careful of falling for him. They hadn't even attended another wedding-related event yet, and Zach was afraid that he was already falling.

Hard, and fast, and painfully.

This was going to hurt.

CHAPTER 18

The hospital had never been so colourful. Scratching at her neck where the collar met her bare skin, Soph debated yet again the merits of winning the stupid bet, before gritting her teeth and deciding to push through it. Pain is gain, and all that crap.

Fortunately, she fit right in amongst the crowd of rowdy healthcare workers, everyone decked out in something red, green, or an eye-watering combination of the two. Christmas lights flashed brightly enough to trigger epilepsy, wrapping around every door frame, free IV stand, and the nurses desks. Chairs had been pushed to the sides of the large waiting room, and a trestle table covered in more alcohol than food drew the attention of most of the guests.

"Here you go!" Finn half-shouted over the latest K-Pop song, handing her a red cup of solo. Sophia had had enough to drink earlier, and just wanted to enjoy the subtle buzz she now felt.

Surprisingly, the last hour had been more enjoyable than she had expected. Over the last few months, she had actually developed good friendships with many of the other staff — Eloise in pathology, Martin in radiology, Catherine the cancer outpatient nurse, to name a few. Where she had expected to be by Finn and Zach's side all night, she had instead been pulled from group to group, gossiping with the nurses and even dancing (reluctantly and shyly at first) with Bridget.

It had been nice. Feeling like she belonged, like she was part of the group here. Without even realising it, they had started to fill the holes in her chest. She felt... full.

Smiling into her cup, Sophia found herself surveying the room, trying to ignore that she was clearly searching for someone. She quickly spotted his tall frame and broad shoulders through a gap between a Santa and an on-call doctor, stethoscope still around her neck, and as if on their own accord, her legs started weaving her through the crowd and towards Zach.

In spite of the hideous sweater, he looked annoyingly handsome, standing opposite a scantily-clad elf wth strawberry blonde hair. Soph lost sight of him behind a stampede of speech pathologists, and when she finally emerged from the crowd a second later, she froze.

The pretty elf had her lips against Zach's ear, which normally would be understandable considering how loud the music had gotten. But her manicured hand was lightly caressing the back of Zach's neck. And her other hand was drawing slow circles on the back of the hand holding his drink.

A heavy, ugly creature had turned her chest into a pool of molten lava.

"Sun — Sophia!" Zach coughed as he finally spotted her. Tucking a loose strand of hair behind her ear, Soph hoped he couldn't see the heat staining her cheeks.

"Hey, Z. I was just…" Just what? 'I was pulled to you like you're my gravity' did not seem appropriate here. "…coming to find you. And Finn. I was thinking of heading home early."

That wasn't a lie, not now that she could still see this woman's hand resting on her best friend's shoulder, could feel her stomach churning for no good reason.

A thought struck her suddenly. What if Zach was keeping their fake dating to fake only because he was interested in someone else? But then why kiss her? Who was this girl?

Screw it, Sophia thought. She was done entertaining trust issues brought about by men who weren't worth a flying fuck.

"I'm Sophia!" she stuck her hand out towards the elf with a bit too much enthusiasm, that most definitely wasn't replicated by the other woman.

"Lidia," she smiled like a snake.

Nef's voice floated through Soph's head. She wasn't being much of a girl's girl right now. And she shouldn't assume anything just because she was... jealous.

Acknowledging the beast in her chest brought a frown to her face, and Lidia must have taken it to be directed at her because she dismissed Soph pretty quickly with a flick of her hair.

"Z, huh? I think I prefer your other nickname more." A playful pout tilted Lidia's mouth.

"I like this one." Zach's tone brooked no argument. "Soph, let me walk you home? I'll just go let Finn know."

Sophia nodded, before realising that this would leave her alone with Lidia. Before she could do anything, Zach had disappeared into the crowd, and Lidia was staring derisively down her nose at her — a feat, considering she was at least two inches shorter, despite the heels.

"Cute matching jumpers," Lidia broke the silence.

"Thanks. It's for a bet."

"You're the techie, right?" Sophia's confusion must have shown on her face. "The one who does all Zach's dirty work in the lab?"

"Oh! I wouldn't call it dirty work. I just do most of the behind the scenes stuff, plus some report writing."

"Like I said, dirty work. Goodness knows Zach has always needed someone to clean up his messes. I used to help him with that, once upon a time."

Girls girl be damned. No one insulted Zach like this.

"Excuse me? Zach is perfectly capable of cleaning up his own mess, not that he makes any. He's been nothing but exceptional to work with."

"Oh, sure," Lidia laughed, reminding Sophia of a hyena. "That's why you're doing most of the writing, right? Or hasn't he told you?"

"Told me what?" This conversation was not going in any imagined direction. Please let Zach be back soon, she silently begged.

"Let's just say his writing is *to die for*. I've got to go, but good luck with the trial! Maybe he'll finally get published this time."

With a finger wave that made her see red, Lidia sauntered away, leaving Soph to try translate whatever the hell that conversation had been.

A hand on her shoulder made her jump, before she recognised Zach's comforting presence behind her.

"Ready to go Sunflower?"

Without realising it, she had leaned back against Zach's chest, savouring his warmth.

"So ready. And I have some tea to spill about this Lidia."

Together, they managed to shuffle out of the hospital, Britney Spears in the background — someone had managed to steal the speaker from Bridget. And it might have been Sophia's overactive imagination, but she swore that Zach's hand grabbed hers for just a little longer than normal as he led her through the crowd. And she might have grabbed his back.

Just a little.

Zach's hand without Sophia's in it was like a line without a hook. The second she pulled away from his grip — and he swore she had been holding his hand as tightly as he was holding hers — he felt empty. Without realising it, Zach's life had become, as Helen Mirren put it in 'Barbie', only good if Barbie looked at him. Or smiled at him. Or touched him.

Really, Sophia could do whatever she wanted and Zach would say thank you just for the privilege of existing near her.

An image of Mira making the whipping action filled his mind. God he hated it when his sister was right.

Staying near enough to brush shoulders, Zach followed Sophia on her path back to her apartment, content with the warm silence.

"Do I have to ask, or will you tell me?" Sophia's soft grin let him know she wouldn't push if he didn't want to.

Sighing, Zach relented. "Yes, she's my ex, no she's clearly not over me, and yes, I am very much over her and have been for the four years since we've split."

"That, I guessed. But that's not what I meant, Z." Her shoulder bumped his again, the light floral perfume she always wore wrapping around him like a blanket.

They kept walking in silence, and Zach was grateful for the time Soph gave him to think. The last thing he had wanted to do earlier was leave her alone with Lidia, so he had rushed back as soon as he had let Finn know they were leaving — and forfeiting their bet to him. Of course Soph would have noticed why Lidia had left so quickly, why she would have given such a sharp parting shot. And of course Sophia was smart enough to know there was a double meaning to it.

"It's a long story," Zach got the words out slowly, unsure how to start. Of everyone, Soph was the person he most wanted to tell. She was also the person he most scared to tell. What if she saw him differently afterwards?

It would be no less than he deserved.

"We have all the time in the world." This time, Sophia took his hand for real, giving a comforting squeeze. "Do you want to go somewhere more comfortable to talk?"

"Are you inviting me home, Sunflower?"

They passed beneath a streetlamp, allowing Zach to appreciate the way her cheeks turned pink at his words.

"Yes. No! I-It's just around the corner. I mean, only if you want to! It's nothing like... I mean... that's what friends do right?"

Laughing, Zach reached out to flick lightly at the crease between her eyebrows, frowning when she swayed slightly to one side.

"You're cute when you're flustered."

"I'm not flustered," Sophia stammered, hands flapping loosely at her sides. She swayed again, and he clocked the subtle limp she had started sporting. She had been wearing those wedges all night...

Just then, Zach spotted a garden wall, about Sophia's waist height. And just because he could, just because he wanted to, he quickly spun around and lifted her by the waist until she was standing on the wall, his hands falling to rest on the curve of her hips.

"Zach!" Sophia squawked, arms fluttering again.

Turning before he let his hands free to their own devices, Zach gave Soph his back and held his arms out. "Hop on, Sunflower."

"What! Why?"

"Because I can see you limping in those shoes. And because I want to."

"But..."

"Soph, I swear if you try to give me a stupid excuse, I'm going to throw you over my shoulder and carry you home that way instead. No one hurts my woman. Not even her shoes."

Fuck, that slipped out. Too late to take anything back, not when it would likely just draw attention to it. So Zach stayed put, arms out patiently, waiting for Sophia's decision.

It came quickly, in the form of her arms winding around his neck, her legs around his hips, until her front was flush against his back, soft strands of her hair tickling the back of his neck. It was far from unpleasant.

"This must be how cowboys feel at a rodeo," Soph muttered.

Zach snorted. "Or how Bella felt when Edward carried her up those trees."

"Does this make me your spider monkey?"

"I guess it does." Without warning, Zach took off at a run, relishing the way Soph's grip tightened around him. Her laugh vibrated through both their chests.

In a few minutes, Zach would tell Soph things that might make her never want anything to do with him again, fake or not.

But for now, he savoured every second.

CHAPTER 19

Four years ago, the Jacobs Medical Centre

Stella was an awfully cute six year old, which did not bode well for Zach. Already, she was tugging at his white coat, pulling his face to hers where she lay in the too-large hospital bed.

"Do I get a jellybean now?" She whispered, the gap between her two front teeth making a slight whistling sound.

"No sweets, honey," her mom interrupted from her chair in the corner. "You'll feel sick like last time."

Stella pouted and flopped back against the pillows. "But it'll help me get better."

Zach forced a smile to his face. Stella had been looking far too small lately. Ribs were becoming visible as she struggled to eat, her eyes — too big in her bald head — were yellowing.

"Sorry Stella-bella-boo," Zach gently squeezed her hand. "You heard your mom."

Stella's eyes widened, and she smothered a delighted grin as Zach slipped her the single pink jellybean he had saved specially for her.

Her mom shook her head, but a smile tugged at her mouth as she pretended to not see Stella shove the treat between her lips.

In this, she and Zach were in cahoots. While it had taken Zach far too long to convince her to let Stella start chemo, they were united in how they just wanted to keep her happy.

Happy, and unaware that she wasn't actually getting better.

"Mrs Jackson, can I talk to you outside? Stella needs some time to rest."

"I'm not tired!" Stella promptly yawned.

"Sleep, honey. I'll be back in five minutes." Mrs Jackson pressed a kiss to her forehead, careful to avoid the various tubes linking her daughter to the IV drip.

Zach waited for Mrs Jackson before drawing the curtains closed around Stella's bed. Their smiles quickly faded.

"Mrs Jackson," he started slowly.

She stopped him with a hand on his arm. "Dr Hayes, I know what you're going to say."

She sniffled, before taking a deep breath. "You said there was a last resort."

Zach nodded, meeting her gaze. A month ago, when the biopsy had come back as terminal, he had suggested enrolling Stella in the latest drug trial, which would use genetically matched STEM cell research to target cancer cells specifically for the patient. Mrs Jackson had already been against chemo, but acquiesced to allowing this as a final option.

"I would like to consent to enrolling Stella in the trial." Her voice didn't waver, and neither did the tears that had started making tracts down her cheeks.

Nodding again, Zach murmured comforting words to Mrs Jackson, before heading to his attending to start the process.

***

"And... done!" Zach pressed the bandaid to Stella's inner elbow as he pulled out the venous catheter a week later. She had been responding well to the new treatment, her appetite returning, but her energy was still abnormally low.

"Can I sleep now?" Stella's eyes were already fluttering closed.

Mrs Jackson stood on the other side of the bed as usual, holding Stella's hand silently. It had been a busy day on the wards, and Zach was exhausted. Somewhere along his twenty four hour call shift, he had misplaced his glasses and his favourite pen. But he couldn't imagine how this mother felt, the relief at seeing her daughter's pain and symptoms eased just slightly.

"Not yet, sweetheart," Mrs Jackson stroked Stella's forehead. "Remember how we're trying to only sleep at night?"

"But I'm so tired, mommy. Please can I sleep?"

Mrs Jackson's face crumpled, and Zach stepped in.

"How about we give you something to help you feel less tired?"

"Like coffee?" Stella perked up.

Zach laughed, and even Mrs Jackson smiled. "Kind of, Stella-bella-boo. You can drink it down with some custard, how about that?"

Stella grinned, tongue poking through her gapped teeth, and Mrs Jackson shot him a look of gratitude.

Leaving the pair in their curtained off area, Zach headed to the hospital's dispensary to grab some modafinil — a common drug used for chemo patients struggling with fatigue.

Squinting at the label on the white box, the words swam in front of his eyes for a second, before clearing. His training came back to him quickly: when checking what drug to use, make sure it's the right patient, right medication, right dosage, right time, and right administration route. And that it hasn't expired.

Flipping the box over to check that the rest of the label matched what he was looking for, his pager beeped loudly.

"Hey, Catherine?" Zach stopped a young nurse who was about to leave the dispensary. "I've got to run to an OR, are you able to please give Stella in room 3B two of these please?"

"Of course! I'll head over now."

"Thanks Catherine, I owe you one!" Zach passed over the box of pills, before power walking to the theatre. He'd check on Stella after the surgery.

***

Present day, Sophia's couch

"I never made it to the theatre." Zach cleared his throat, eyes stinging. He couldn't look Sophia in the eye. "Catherine had gone straight away, as promised. And Stella had always been so good at taking her meds that she never complained that I forgot to mention the custard."

Stella's face, her wide blue eyes and the soft tufts of blonde hair that had just started growing back, drifted across his vision.

"I'm dyslexic, Soph. And I've always managed it well, always been extra careful when it comes to the medications and prescribing, but this one day, this one moment, I didn't check properly. And I gave Stella methadone by accident instead of modafinil."

Something warm and wet dropped down his cheek, but Zach didn't wipe it away. He barely registered that Sophia's hand was on his arm, that somewhere between entering her apartment and sitting down in the living room she had given him a hand-crochet blanket.

"Methadone is contraindicated for chemo patients. Stella had a heart attack just as I entered the scrubbing room. And I had to tell Mrs Jackson what I had done."

"Oh Zach..." Sophia moved to hug him, but Zach shifted away.

"I killed her, Sophia. It was my fault. That's why I don't write my own reports, that's why all I've focused on for the last few years has been getting approval for this drug trial. It's why I needed you on the team."

His words tasted bitter, a long overdue confession that would have brought him to his knees if he hadn't already been sitting down.

"Zach," Sophia's hands were on his face, turning his head so he had no choice but to meet her gaze at last. "It wasn't your fault."

He stared at her incredulously. Did she not just hear what he had told her? Maybe she was just in denial, like had initially been when he found out. Zach was ready to explain again, to make her see she was friends with someone who had accidentally murdered a child, when she cut him off again.

"Listen to me. There are hundreds of other staff who were there that day who are equally responsible. The pharmacists who didn't double check what was being removed from the dispensary and for whom. Catherine, who should have asked why this medication was being used for Stella instead of blindly giving it to her.

Any other nurse or doctor or allied health whatever could have checked, the same way you did. And any other professional would have checked the same way you did anyway, before heading off to answer a page from the OR.

It was a terrible, terrible accident, and it could have happened to anyone. But from what I've seen, it doesn't make you a murderer. It makes you a better doctor."

Sophia was breathing heavily, on her knees on the couch facing him. Her hair was starting to frizz from the humidity in the apartment, and her skin was flushed, showing off the freckles under her eye.

She wasn't finished with her rant, either.

"I don't say this callously, and I don't say this to take away from what happened or diminish the severity of it — for you or for Stella's family. But I'm guessing you're leaving out what you did afterwards, and are focusing too hard on your guilt?"

No one had ever seen straight through him before, had understood the core of what pained him so much.

"I went to the funeral. The coffin... it was so small. It had been painted pink. It looked like her favourite jellybean…" Zach's voice was hoarse, and the tears were still flowing, slower now. "I paid for all of it. I insisted."

"And you still donate yearly to the Starlight Foundation."

"I — yes. How did you know?"

Sophia looked slightly sheepish. "I told Nef about you and she did some internet stalking. You were at a charity ball for the foundation in Dubai a few years ago, and her fiancé is friends with Danilo, the guy who ran it. He mentioned seeing you there."

He often forgot that Sophia's best friend (other than himself) was engaged to one of the most successful modern archeologists of the century.

"Yeah. I donate yearly."

"And I'm willing to bet you complied with all hospital protocol and went to all the necessary counselling sessions."

"Of course." What was Sophia trying to say here?

"My point is that you did everything right. And that you're a better doctor for it today, because of the care and vigilance you show your patients. And you're not the kind of person to shun therapy, which means that there's a reason this still haunts you today."

Swiping a hand over his eyes, Zach cleared his throat. The tears were gone, and the ever-present guilt in his stomach felt slightly lighter now. And despite what he'd revealed, Sophia was still looking at him the same way. Like he meant something to her.

"I wrote to Mrs Jackson about the new trial, how I was finally doing it and how I would like her permission to dedicate the paper to Stella if it ever got published."

Sophia had moved closer next to him, and now seemed to be holding her breath.

"She never forgave you, did she? That's what still bothers you so much?"

"Actually... she did."

CHAPTER 20

"Isn't that a good thing?" Sophia tilted her head to the side. Why would Zach be upset that he had finally been granted forgiveness?

Zach was trembling beside her, though she didn't think he had noticed. When he had told her he wanted to talk at hers, she hadn't realised it would be this serious, or that it would affect him so much.

Her heart broke for him and the burden he had been carrying for so long.

"How am I supposed to finally let this go? What kind of doctor, what kind of person am I without this guilt? I know I should have moved on years ago, but what if I make a mistake again and my dyslexia hurts another patient? If I accept her forgiveness, I'm scared that I'll become complacent."

Tears were slipping down Zach's face again. "I know death is part of the job, especially for oncology. But I don't think I could survive a second Stella."

Sophia did the only thing she could think of. Still on her knees on the couch, she slid an arm around Zach's neck and leant forward. She flicked out her tongue, catching a salty tear in its track. Another tear. Then the other cheek.

"What are you doing?" Zach was whispering again, but he sounded curious, not disgusted, so she continued pressing soft open mouthed kisses over his cheeks.

"Comforting you? I can stop if it's too weird. When I was eleven and my dog died, I cried to Nef about who would lick my tears away now. She did this for me. She kissed away my tears."

"Keep going," Zach's voice was like gravel.

His stubble was so rough compared to his smooth skin, the contrast causing a delicious friction against Sophia's lips as she continued to pepper Zach's face with gentle pecks. A small groan slipped out of Zach, so soft she never would have heard it if she hadn't placed her head just then so that his mouth was right by her ear.

There were no more tears, and with that realisation came a second: somehow, Soph had ended up nearly straddling Zach on the couch, her crotch just inches away from his.

A roaring filled her ears as she fought back filthy, impossible thoughts. Of her dragging her nails over the cotton of Zach's briefs, riding his face until she squirted all over him, marking him as hers.

She'd never had these thoughts about Eliot.

Her breathing hitched, but she didn't move from her spot, scared that if she did she'd draw attention to just how not friendly they were sitting.

"Sophia," Zach's voice was so low she didn't know how she understood him.

"Zach." They were close enough that they were breathing each other's air. If Soph leant forward, would Zach kiss her back?

She felt like Icarus, but god, she was ready to burn for him. He could rip the waxy feathers from her body himself and she'd smile through the pain, just grateful that it was his hands on her.

She could count the flecks of green in his brown eyes at this distance. His right eye had seven. That was a lucky number, according to her grandmother.

"Sunflower..." Zach shifted his hips minutely, and Sophia was ready to pray to every god she had ever heard of.

Zach's phone started vibrating. He ignored it. His hands moved to squeeze Soph's hips, and she swore she could stay suspended in this moment forever. Carefully, she looped her hands around the back of Zach's neck properly, wrapping the soft loose curls at the base of his neck around her fingers.

They noticed they were still wearing their sweaters at the same time.

Zach's phone buzzed again, and this time he grabbed for it, muting it without moving his eyes off hers. She followed the bob of his Adam's apple with her eyes, wishing it was her tongue.

"You know," his voice twined around her like shadows in the dark living room. Only her favourite soft lamp was on, casting them both in a golden hour of their own making. "I let Finn win the bet."

"Ok..." Where was he going with this?

"You can take your sweater off now."

"I'm not wearing anything under it though. I hate layers."

"I know."

The full force of Zach's words hit Soph at once, and she felt a rush of dampness as she realised what Zach was suggesting.

It was like a choose your own adventure moment, and Soph knew exactly where each option would lead. And she didn't really want to take the safe road anymore.

She reached for the hem of her jumper, shifting back only enough so she'd have room to move her arms over her head.

And then the fire alarm went off.

Nef was in disbelief. "You got cockblocked by a fire alarm."

Throwing up an arm, Soph fell back against her pillows. Nef had come over the next day for a long overdue catch up, and the two friends were now slumped over Sophia's plump mattress, toe nails freshly painted and an eclectic mix of snacks scattered around the room.

"The universe is conspiring me against me, I swear. The one time it felt like we were actually moving beyond just friends, and in a healthy way too." Soph stared up at her ceiling, where plastic glow in the dark stars had been stuck up and left behind by the previous tenant. She hadn't even considered taking them down.

"Maybe it's a sign, Nef." Soph sighed heavily. "Nothing good has ever come from pining after a fake date."

Nef threw a pillow at her face, hitting Soph with a muffled thwomp. "Tell that to Hollywood."

"You just made your own point — this shit only happens in movies. Not real life."

Nef sat up on her heels and made her voice a high pitched falsetto. "'He gripped my hips and I could count the flecks in his eyes and I touched his hair and I was almost straddling him —'"

It was Soph's turn to throw the pillow. It sailed straight past Nef, overturning a packet of doritos that was open on her desk instead.

"I do *not* sound like that —"

Nef cackled, swatting at Soph's thigh. "Trust me, honey, I'm just as mad about the fire alarm as you. I need those juicy details!"

Soph felt her cheeks heat.

"You don't get to be embarrassed, missy. Remember how much you made me tell you when I met Xander?"

"It's not that," Soph grumbled. Swiping another pillow from the pile on her bed, she shoved her face into it. "I'm having some really dirty thoughts."

"Girl, now you HAVE to spill. Are you thinking about finally trying bondage? Cause let me tell you about this thing Xander did last night —"

"I will stop you right there, Nef." Soph grinned as she peeked out from behind her fluffy shield. Nef was cross legged now, an exaggerated look of patience painting her features.

Sighing, Soph decided to come clean. After all, Nef was the one person (aside from Zach) who she would always tell everything to.

"When I was with Eliot, things were pretty... vanilla."

Nef nodded, familiar with Soph's doubts in the bedroom from her past relationship.

"Obviously, I still can't remember my night with Zach, but every time I think about him that way..."

"Spit it out, Soph. How kinky are we talking?"

"I want to be the one in control."

Soph's confession rolled around the quiet room. Nef's face didn't give anything away.

"How in control?" Nef said at last. "Again, no judgement from me, ever, but just so I know what page you're on."

"Like, I want to make him sit at my feet and worship me. And I want to edge him so badly then ruin his orgasm. And... other things."

"Damn, Soph." Nef whistled slowly. "I never pegged you for a femdom. Omg. Pegging. Is that also something you want to try? What about CBT?"

"CB-what? And I don't know! I've never done any of this before, or even thought about it before. There's something about Zach that just..." Soph let out a strangled noise. "It just feels right to take care of him that way, I guess. And I feel safe to do that with him, like me being in control makes both of us feel better, at least in the bedroom."

"Well, I always say don't knock it 'til you've tried it. Why don't you go for it?"

Soph deflated. "I don't want to complicate things. I'm definitely over Eliot now, but I still feel like it's too soon. Plus we just agreed to fake date, I can't go back on that so quickly. Can I?"

The hope in her voice must have been clear as day, because Nef manoeuvred gracelessly until she was next to Soph against the pillows, head on her shoulder.

"There's still a month until the wedding. No harm in fantasising in the meantime, and see how things turn out."

Soph nodded slowly.

"Head up, love," Nef poked her in the ribs, smirking. "I doubt the man who gripped your hips and suggested you strip is going to go anywhere too quickly. Fire alarm or not."

CHAPTER 21

Zach didn't think he had ever used his hand so rigorously in a single month before. Every day was filled now with thoughts of Sophia — when they ate lunch together, when she stayed after hours in his office or her lab to write up the methodology, when she visited him (and Finn) in the wards to bring little gift boxes to the patients in their trial while they braved their weekly injections.

He had tried so hard to think about anything, anyone else. But every time he thought about using an app or visiting a bar, flashes of buttery yellow and sky blue would make him freeze in place.

And then have a very cold shower.

The rehearsal dinner for Eliot and Olivia's wedding was officially in three days now, and the snow was really coming down. The 'poor weather plan' had been enacted, so to save the poor guests from having to track to and from the venue at La Jolla Hotel, the spouses-to-be had booked everyone in to their own room for the night.

Which meant that amongst the romantic, snow-dusted streets and plush bedding of the luxury hotel and spa venue, Zach would be sharing a bed with Sophia as they prepared for her ex's wedding.

Thank god New Years Eve had been a night shift — holiday pay and the opportunity to steer clear of Soph, lest he do something stupid. Like kiss her. Or be forced to watch as she kissed someone else.

Their evening together after the Christmas party flashed through Zach's memories in slow motion. Soph had felt so soft and supple beneath his hands, yet so strong. So... dominant.

He had liked it. A lot.

Today was not the time to be thinking about how good it would feel to let Sophia have her way with him again. Dragging a hand down his stubble, which had grown out a bit over the last few days, he turned back to the task at hand: finalising patient follow up so that results could start being graphed.

Zach loved this part of the trial. It felt like a Friday night in undergrad, when the weekend was guaranteed to be free and all that was left was this small bit of work to power through. The second everyone was followed up and accounted for, outliers could be removed and he could give the data to Rhys, their statistician, to play around with while Soph started the discussion and conclusion part of the report.

By the time September rolled around again, they would have final results, time to edit and polish their report, and then could submit for publication while applying for another grant to start phase three.

For reasons Zach didn't care to explore further, he had come down to Sophia's lab after hours to go through the data. He loved his office, and the bright windows it had, but something about Sophia's desk under the fluorescent lights, covered in fake plants and neatly labeled pink and orange binders, calmed him.

Plus, most of the researchers from other labs had gone home by now, while his office was off the main corridor and was a permanent thoroughfare of health workers regardless of the time or day.

Zach could practically hear Mira's snicker in his head, tutting to him about poor excuses.

Rubbing a hand through his hair as though to disperse any intrusive thoughts, Zach settled back into the rolling chair to keep working. He spent another hour like this, which turned into two, then three. Around nine pm, Zach finally glanced up from his laptop and decided to call it a night.

Grabbing his phone, he ignored the text from Angelo, RSVP'd to Danilo's invite to the latest charity gala (scheduled for end of February with the option for a plus one), then, like the compulsion it was, opened his text chain with Sophia.

The last text had been a series of photos Soph had sent him from last weekend. Instead of their usual karaoke night, they had decided to try the new laser tag place that had opened around the block. Finn had pulled out last minute, so he and Sophia had spent two hours alternating between teaming up against a group of friends half their age, and annihilating each other 'battle of the sexes' style. Zach couldn't remember the last time he had had so much fun.

The photos were some of his new prized possessions. Three sets of digital Photo Booth pictures showed him and Sophia in various poses. The first set, they were smiling normally before making stupid faces at the camera and laughing. In the second set, Zach was licking Soph's cheek, her own face set permanently in a look of pure disgust and indignation, before she pushed Zach out of the frame in the bottom photo.

The last set was his favourite though. He had already gotten them printed at Target, and was planning to frame them as a birthday gift for Soph later this year. This set of three started with Soph trying to lick Zach in retribution, followed by them cracking up, Soph's face hidden in the crook of his neck while he threw his head back, eyes closed mid-cackle.

The last photo was the best though. Soph was smiling widely, eyes closed, both arms wrapped around his neck while she faced the camera. Her hair was out and shining under the lights, the sequins on her dress sparkling. Zach had a hand around her waist to support her, loose curls and the sharp profile of his jaw in view while he planted a sound kiss on her cheek.

For such a chaste kiss, something about the photo hinted that things maybe weren't as platonic as they seemed. It was written in the tighter than usual grip of Sophia's hand on his collared shirt, in the possessive way he wrapped his hand around her waist, in the way they both seemed to turn towards each other like magnets even though they faced the camera.

The hope, imaginary or not, was almost too much to bear. But Zach couldn't look away.

Sophia had a terrible, wonderful idea. Rehearsal dinner was tomorrow, and she and Zach were planning to leave together early in the morning to drive up to the hotel. True to form, she was already packed, her dress hanging under an opaque protective cover on a hook on her bedroom door.

Her idea consumed her. It was reckless, and selfish, and so outlandish it might just work. But she and Zach had been walking a precipice for months now, and if she didn't do something soon they would crash and burn.

Whipping out her phone as she treaded a path into her living room rug, she sent the text, then promptly threw her phone across the room, narrowly missing her favourite flower vase.

I'M NERVOUS ABOUT TOMORROW, she had sent.

This was true.

I THINK WE SHOULD PRACTICE BEING A COUPLE, TO MAKE SURE WE'RE CONVINCING.

This was a lie. They were so damn convincing it took half of her day to remember that they weren't actually dating, and they weren't even pretending to be a couple outside of the wedding stuff. Finn, Bridget, Angelo, and even Ailish from HR had asked her about their relationship status — Ailish mostly because she wanted the necessary forms filled out to prevent a conflict of interest if that was the case. The others were just nosy.

Across the room, her phone buzzed loudly from its new home behind the couch.

Sophia collected it with a sigh, trying not to inhale the mountain of dust that lived beneath the plush cushions of the small sofa. Relief that it was undamaged lasted less than a millisecond before she saw Zach's response.

I AGREE. 8PM, MY PLACE. I'LL PICK YOU UP.

Tingles erupted through Sophia's body, hair standing on end on her arms as she read, then reread, the text. Zach had said yes.

They could both pretend that this was exactly as written — practice. Pretend. Make-believe. She knew they both knew better.

As Sophia went to get ready for tonight, she couldn't help but wonder if the line they were walking was any safer than before. Or if she and Zach were both about to fall off the deep end.

Either way, they were in this together. And had both fallen into tonight's plans, hook, line, and sinker.

CHAPTER 22

Time seemed to run like liquid sand until evening finally arrived, and still Sophia didn't let out the breath she felt she had been holding since she had sent her earlier text.

Every inch of her had been shined and polished to perfection, just the right amount of perfume sprayed at her neck and wrists — and inner ankles. Though that was likely getting too far ahead of herself. When Soph had suggested she and Zach 'practice' being a couple, she hadn't really had anything in mind aside from an overwhelming compulsion to finally do something about the heavy air of anticipation that seemed to permanently engulf them.

The one goal for tonight? Don't forget it tomorrow.

Punctual as ever, Zach rang her doorbell at eight on the dot.

"You could have waited in the car," Soph smiled up at him, hair still damp from her shower. Zach tugged gently on a loose strand hanging over her eye.

"It's so much darker when it's wet," he rasped. "Like honey."

Doing her best not to stare at the way his fingers toyed with her waves, Sophia made a noncommittal sound of agreement.

"Being wet also means I shouldn't stay too long in the cold. Let's get going?" She made to move out the door, but Zach's arm shot out in front of her, barring the way.

"Where's your suitcase?"

"In my bedroom? I'll grab it tomorrow."

"Why?"

Soph wanted nothing more than to smooth her fingers over the adorable frown between Zach's brows. "Because after we... after tonight, I'll come back and you'll pick me up tomorrow? Like planned?"

She really needed to stop phrasing everything like a question.

With the same lightning reflexes as before, Zach manoeuvred between Soph and the door, long legs eating up the distance between the entry way and her bedroom. Before Sophia could speak, he was back — her suitcase in one hand, her dress and matching shoes dangling from its coat hanger in his other.

"You didn't think you could proposition me and then leave, did you, Sunflower?"

"Proposition?" Soph squeaked. "I'm not, I didn't..." did she?

"Don't worry, Soph. I promise we can treat it like research. I know you didn't mean anything by it, right?"

"Right." Except it wasn't right at all. And Sophia was too much of a coward, too selfish, to refute anything. No, all she would do is exploit her best friend for intimacy while denying her feelings because god-forbid she move on from her past relationship too quickly.

She could have sworn disappointment flashed in Zach's eyes, but he had started walking to the car before she could try interpret it any further.

Following along on unsteady legs, the car ride was comfortable despite the atmosphere of swirling anticipation. They both knew they were about to cross a line.

Sophia just wasn't sure yet if she wanted to cross back over after.

Zach's place was a modest two bedroom town house near Balboa park. Sophia hadn't known what to expect, but walking through the well-kept front garden to the pink-washed brick entryway, she could see pieces of Zach and his family throughout.

A short hallway led into an open-plan living space with a rectangular dining room table and a dated but clean kitchen. Family photos lined the wall between the couch and tv, showing various poses of two similar looking kids with gapped teeth, sometimes in their parent's arms, sometimes at milestones like birthdays or a graduation. Soph had never met Mira before, but recognised her immediately from a head shot of her from Prom, next to a beautiful silver menorah.

"You're Jewish?" She was surprised he hadn't brought it up before.

"Only when there's food involved. My Safta used to say though that just because god doesn't exist, doesn't mean we can get out of going to Synagogue."

Soph grinned, trailing her fingers over the soft blankets that littered two velvety couches. It was a beautiful home — clearly lived in but tidy, smelling faintly like Zach's cologne and a lighter, more fruity scent she couldn't place. Walking into the kitchen, she glimpsed the three doors further down the hall that continued at the end of the room, likely the bedrooms and bathroom.

Vaguely, an odd sense of deja vu overcame her, and she remembered that although this was the first time seeing his place, it wasn't her first time visiting. An evening from many months ago flashed through her mind, of a silver dress pooled on a bedroom floor and of strong, muscled arms tangled around her. Of running blindly for the front door and a taxi when she got her wits about her.

"Mira sometimes stays here when she visits. She only lives half an hour away but it's still nice to have her here."

"I always wondered what it would be like to have siblings."

Waving a hand across his face, Zach smirked. "Pros and cons, Sunflower."

Without noticing, he had followed her into the kitchen and retrieved two margarita glasses from the cupboard.

"I don't have the nice glasses at the moment," he said apologetically. "Mira stole them. Wine?"

"God, yes."

They sipped in silence for a few minutes while Soph surveyed Zach's home.

"So what kind of practice were you thinking, Sunflower?"

Sophia nearly choked on her drink.

"Wow," she sputtered. "You really get straight to the point."

Zach's face didn't shift from his serious expression, heavy eyebrows framing eyes dark with obvious lust. "Our previous ground rules stated kissing only."

Soph nodded, gaze dropping to Zach's full lips. She remembered *very* clearly.

"I would like to amend that." When Sophia's eyes snapped to his, Zach corrected himself. "Just for tonight, that is. While we practice."

There was something biting in the way he uttered the last word, as though practicing was far from the front of his mind.

"I'm open to amendments." Her voice came out breathier than normal, and she self consciously tucked her hair behind her ears again.

"I propose everything on the table except for sex."

If Soph had been taking a sip again, she would have choked for sure. "Like first base to third?"

"If baseball terms are what'll help make it clearer for you, then sure."

Sophia cocked her head to the side, pretending to think about it. Like she hadn't already thought about it since the second she sent that text.

"Deal. But!" Zach's cocky smirk faltered for a split second. "I need you to choose a safe word."

"Why do *I* need to choose, Sunflower?"

"Because I'm going to be the one in charge here if we do this. And if we've done this before, even though I can't remember, I have a feeling you really enjoyed being a good boy for me. So choose."

CHAPTER 23

Zach could feel his cock straining at the seam of his pants. Sophia was dead right.

He had tried his best to block out their first — and so far only — night together; it had been too good to be true. Sophia had been a goddess, and Zach had been more than willing to worship her while on his knees.

While he had been fully prepared to explain to Soph what he wanted, he was also grateful that some part of her seemed to instinctually remember what he liked.

"Your safe word, Z?" Soph cocked an eyebrow, and damn if her growing sexual confidence didn't make him impossibly harder.

Clearing his throat, Zach rumbled out his chosen word. "Lemons."

"Good boy," Sophia purred.

Heat rushed through Zach, pooling in his stomach as his balls tightened. He could barely feel the glass of wine he was still holding. All his senses were trained instead on the magnificent woman in front of him, who was ever so slowly unbuttoning her loose cardigan while simultaneously slipping off her flats.

"What do you want to practice first, *girlfriend*?" Zach's voice was octaves lower than normal. Ignoring how right the term sounded when applied to his best friend, he continued. "I'm sure the guests would be surprised if we weren't comfortable kissing."

Sophia's eyes glinted. "Then I guess you should show me how you're gonna kiss me, *boyfriend*."

That was it. All restraint snapped and Zach surged froward, glass discarded somewhere on the kitchen bench, his only priority being Sophia and her mouth.

God, her mouth.

She tasted like strawberry lip balm. Groaning, Zach pulled her flush to his chest, devouring her soft lips like a man starved. His Sunflower was so perfect, so soft, so pliant under his hands and his tongue. He remembered how good she tasted elsewhere, how much he had blocked out about her in order to function while seeing her every day.

Sophia was gripping his hair like a lifeline, the light pain as she tugged making his cock twitch. Gently, he swept his tongue across her bottom lip, nipping it as she opened for him at last.

Suddenly, Sophia pushed at his chest and they broke apart, flushed and panting. Soph's lips were slightly swollen, and Zach knew his blown pupils likely mirrored hers.

"I," Sophia gasped, arms still twined around his neck. "I think the guests will find that pretty believable."

Zach rubbed his thumb against the apple of her cheek, before sliding his hand around the back of her neck and tugging her towards him again. Capturing her mouth in another steep kiss, Zach pulled away again.

"Anything else you want to practice, Sunflower?"

He loved how her cheeks pinked every time he used her nickname. Sophia grinned wickedly, as though remembering who was leading this strange dance of theirs.

"You know, I think you should kiss me again. After all, this is for research, and for accuracy's sake we should repeat things at least three times —"

Zach was kissing her again before she could finish. Three times could go to hell. Zach had plans for tonight, and they involved taking the 'at least' part of her statement and multiplying it as many times as possible. Surely Sophia felt how right this was? How perfectly they fit together?

There was no way she would have suggested this 'practice session' if she didn't feel the same way he did.

A niggling doubt voiced itself in the back of his mind as Sophia licked into his mouth, her tongue turning his knees molten as he gripped her waist for support. What if this was just practice? Just a rebound, a distraction before her ex got married?

No, Zach told himself as he manoeuvred Sophia towards his bedroom, not breaking their frantic kisses. She told you this wasn't a distraction, wasn't because of Eliot, he reminded himself as he moved to her neck, relishing the loud moan Sophia let out against his ear.

In his haste to get Sophia to his room, Zach hadn't realised that she wasn't holding his hair anymore. Instead, pleasure tore through like an avalanche as he felt her nails scrape against the v of his hips, dipping dipping dipping under the layers of fabric until they were gripping him right where he needed it, just like all those months ago.

Except this time, he never wanted her to stop.

Zach let out a loud moan, and Sophia swallowed the sound as she turned the tables, pushed *him* up against the bedroom door as she kicked it closed without looking.

Everything was so hot so smooth so perfect, the rhythm hard and fast and unbelievably *good*, and he couldn't wait to feel everything, everywhere, as many times as Soph needed it.

He was hers to use as she wished.

But first, he needed to prove to her that he meant it.

"Sunflower," he gasped against her lips, "I need to taste you again."

"Are my kisses not enough for you?"

"Nothing about you is ever enough. I want more." Zach swallowed, Adam's apple bobbing in his throat. Sophia tracked the movement with her eyes, her hands drawing enticing circles on his lower abs now.

"So greedy for me," she purred.

Yes. He was going to *devour* her —

Sophia had removed her thick stockings, her checkered skirt discarded haphazardly by her flats. That wouldn't do at all. No, it would be extremely ungentlemanly of him to let her undress without assistance.

Stepping closer, chest heaving, Zach dropped to his knees in front of Sophia, who had now been backed towards the edge of his large bed. He pressed a kiss to the top of her soft stomach, to the edge of her hip, to the top of her inner thigh. Slowly, torturously, letting his tongue dart out to steal a taste each time. Gripping the hem of her long sleeve shirt, he tugged it upwards, and Sophia completed the movement for him until she was standing naked in front of him.

"No underwear or bra?" Zach's voice was hoarse.

Sophia winked, dropping back on the bed and spreading her legs, giving Zach an unobstructed view of his new favourite meal.

"I thought you liked surprises."

"I really, really, do." Zach growled and edged forward, nearly crawling in his urgency to get closer. Dipping his head, he inhaled deeply at the sweet, strong scent of his woman. *His* woman. His best friend.

"Before I start, I need to hear you say you're ok with this."

"Z, I wouldn't be in this position if I wasn't." The eye roll was evident.

"Sunflower, I need to hear you say it." Desperation bled into his voice. "Because once I start, I won't be able to stop. I'm going to take my time making you shake, making you cum. I'm going to make sure every time you close your eyes you see me on my knees in front of you. You own me, love."

The endearment slipped out of him, and he couldn't bring himself to care. It was true. He already knew Sophia held his whole heart. This had never really felt fake to him.

"Zach." Soph's voice was firm, and she tugged on his hair to the point of pain until he met her gaze. "I am very, very ok with this."

And with that, she dragged him forwards and straight between her legs.

CHAPTER 24

Nothing in the world existed except this. Zach's large, strong hands wedging her thighs apart like it was nothing. His rough, short stubble scraping her hypersensitive inner thighs. His hot, wet tongue licking, sucking, *feasting*, on her core.

There was no other word for it, what he was doing.

Sophia forgot that this was supposed to be practice, supposed to be fake. Forgot that she was in charge here. She undulated against Zach's unforgiving strokes, bucked as he dragged his teeth lightly over her clit, whimpered when he added one finger, then two, deep inside her in delicious, pumping strokes.

It really didn't take long. One second, Zach was pressing one hand against her lower stomach as he licked her slit from bottom to top, and the next he was sucking her clit between his lips and everything was white and hot and too much, too much, too much.

She collapsed back on the bed, not even aware of how far her back had lifted off the bed, how she had squeezed Zach's head between her thighs as she came on his face.

Panting, but wearing a self-satisfied smirk, Zach looked up at her, chin still wet with her slick. He was the most attractive man she had ever seen in her life.

Wiping his mouth with the back of his hand, Zach grinned. "Was that enough for you, Sunflower?"

His words from earlier echoed back to her.

Never enough.

Sitting up and hiding her shaking legs, she rubbed a soothing circle over Zach's chest.

"Your turn," she grinned an innocent, pretty smile. And relished the flash of eagerness she got in response.

"Lie down," Soph commanded. She shifted her legs, flipping so she was parallel with the bed now. Zach clambered up beside her, laying down on his back against the corduroy navy doona.

Soph ran her gaze over him, his hair disheveled and more curly than usual, mouth still glistening with remnants of her. He was still fully dressed.

She raised an eyebrow as she glanced at his crotch. "That looks painful."

"It is," Zach said against gritted teeth.

The cold metal of his zipper caught at her fingers as she pulled, and Zach lifted his hips to help her tug the rest of his garments away. Shirt, pants, underwear, until he was completely, gloriously, bare.

Sophia swallowed, hard.

"You never told me you…"

Zach grinned roguishly. "Did you think I was a straight laced puritan? Its cause I'm a doctor, isn't it."

She couldn't stop staring. Zach had always been gorgeous, and goodness knew she struggled to keep her eyes off his muscular frame for too long, the carved abs and deep v line that she could now admit she had fantasised about constantly. But she couldn't look away from the thick black lines decorating half of his lower left hip bone, outlining a series of hyper-realistic roses.

"It's called a tattoo, Sunflower." Zach's voice was full of laughter, like he was pleased to have surprised her with this.

"I know what a tattoo is, smart ass. How did you not tell me about this?"

"Technically, you knew and just forgot." Zach smirked. "But if it helps, I clearly remember how much you told me you liked it."

"God you're such a guy sometimes," Soph muttered, smiling.

"Nice of you to notice."

Cocky Zach was hot. But Zach was not in control here. She was. And while his tattoo was gorgeous, it was not enough to distract her from the long, hard span of his cock, jutting in a curve towards his belly button and practically aching to be touched.

Sophia shuffled between his legs, pushing his knees apart with her own until she was able to comfortably lie down on her stomach, hands bracketing Zach's hips similarly to how he had held hers just a few minutes ago.

Using her nails, she scraped gently at his upper thighs as she pressed a wet kiss to the side of his groin, relishing the gasp she got in return.

"You gonna use your tongue for me, Sunflower?"

"Only if you beg for it, baby."

Only their breathing filled the room, heavy, uneven pants while Soph continued to trace circles on Zach's skin.

"Please," he barely whispered. "Please use your mouth, your tongue. I need you to —"

Zach had barely finished speaking before Sophia had swallowed him whole. Her jaw stretched, almost locked, as she opened herself for him, lapping at his cock until he was hitting the back of her throat. She could feel her mascara start to run as she forced herself deeper, determined to make his begging worth every second.

She couldn't pretend it wasn't partly for selfish reasons. He tasted so good, just the right amount of saltiness and that male musk she had come to associated with him. She wanted to wind him up and drink him down forever. She could live on the sounds of his moans, on the way he bucked his hips violently when she ever so lightly ran her teeth up his length as she pulled back.

"More, please Sunflower, *more*," Zach bucked again and this time Sophia added her hand, twisting at the base of his shaft with every dip of her head. Zach had twined his own hands in her already mussed-up hair, and seemed torn between running his hands through her strands soothingly or pulling himself deeper into her.

Pulling herself off him with a wet popping sound, Sophia surged for his mouth without stopping the motion of her hand. His groans tasted almost as sweet as he did.

"Soph," Zach gasped. "I'm so close. Please, I'm almost there."

"Shhh," she murmured against his lips, kissing him again, biting sharply on his lower lip before licking the hurt to soothe it. "Just a little longer. You can hold it, right baby? For me?"

Moving back down between his thighs, Sophia resumed her position, swirling her tongue around Zach's throbbing head while swapping hands so she could pump him harder, faster. She could feel his balls tightening and knew he was close.

Looking up for a split second, Soph caught Zach's gaze. He looked like a god, splayed out on the sheets for her, eyes closed, one hand tucked behind his head and the other in a fist, knuckle held tightly between his teeth. He looked like he was in pain; the most exquisite, delicious pain.

Sophia practically saw the shift in him before she felt it.

With a loud gasp and another snap of his hips, Zach was pulling Sophia off him and roughly dragging his own hand over his length in a punishing grip.

"That's right," she practically cooed as she settled further onto her stomach. "Come for me, baby. Paint me."

Her words undid him, and Zach cried out, his spend coming in waves that landed on her forehead, her cheeks, the corner of her open mouth.

Chest heaving, Zach fell back on his elbows, eyes wide and staring as though he couldn't believe what they'd just done.

Satisfied and smug, Sophia flicked out her tongue to show him the small amount of his seed that had landed in her mouth. And promptly swallowed.

"Fuck me," Zach tilted his head back with a groan as Sophia smiled and reached for the tissues by his bed.

She winked, the cat that got the cream - literally. "Maybe if you beg."

CHAPTER 25

Maybe it was the novelty of it all, or maybe it was the comfort of simply being close to his best friend, but there was (unfortunately) no begging after that. There was only a fast, sweet descent into a dreamless sleep, cut short by a shrieking alarm.

For a moment, Zach felt pleasantly weightless, high on the endorphins from the night before.

"Zach," a soft whisper tickled his ear, followed by a gentle touch curving over his bare chest.

"Mmm," he groaned, turning towards the owner of the hand.

The whisper came again, louder this time. "Zach, we've got to get up."

Memories started computing again. Up. Rehearsal dinner. Sophia. Sophia in his bed. Sophia naked in his bed.

Well. *Something* was now up.

Gathering his strength silently, Zach flipped with lightning speed, pulling Soph deeper into the bedsheets and manoeuvring himself on top of her.

She looked absolutely edible like this: flushed, full mouth parted slightly in surprise, her yellow gold hair tussled from sleep. And of course it didn't hurt that she was still undressed, her soft, warm body pressed against his own.

"We should really get up..." Her voice was hoarser than normal, and Zach wanted nothing more than to lick deep into her mouth, claim her body again and again.

She was his. She had always been his, his best friend, but last night only proved that now she was his in every the way, the same way he knew without a single doubt that she owned him, body and soul.

"Soph," Zach kissed the corner of her mouth, the slope of her brow, revelling in the low moan she let slip. "I know we said last night was practice. But what if we made this something real?"

Sophia's blue eyes were wide open now. Before she could speak, Zach rushed on, words spilling unbridled from his mouth.

"Please, Sophia. I'll beg if I have to, and I know you said you don't want anything until you're over Eliot completely, but it's killing me to wait on the sidelines anymore. It's going to kill me now that I've touched you, tasted you, to stand next to you and pretend you mean the world to me when you actually do."

He was panting now, his confession unbidden and raw. Not bearing to see Soph's expression, he turned away and started pulling on boxers, giving her space to process.

"Z, I —"

That. Fucking. Alarm.

Startled like a doe, Soph leaped from the bed and started grabbing frantically at clothes, trying to cover herself at the same time. Mumbling something about the bathroom, she ducked out of the room, avoiding his gaze.

Tipping his head back with a groan, Zach swore to himself to never press snooze again.

***

The car ride to the rehearsal dinner was possibly more awkward than he had anticipated, though it felt rather one sided. Sophia spent the hour chattering non-stop over her playlist about the research project and how much she reckoned the couple had spent on the wedding, while Zach smiled, nodded, and pretended to ignore the fact that he had ripped his heart out for this woman who hadn't accepted or rejected it yet.

Now, he liked to think that being a doctor meant he wasn't stupid. So if Sophia decided that she wanted to pretend like last night and this morning hadn't happened, he would too. If Sophia decided to acknowledge that it had happened and rejected him anyway, he would be the son his mother had raised, and would graciously ensure that he was the best possible friend she had without breaching any boundaries or pining over her like a lost puppy.

No, the pining would only be in private, and only for a few days before he picked himself up and got on with his day, because he would rather burn in hell than be the man who was only friends with a woman because he wanted a relationship.

The hotel they pulled up to was gorgeous — all sandstone and marble floors with red tiled roofs, manicured lawns that looked way too lush for the time of year, and fountains spotted around the driveway, empty for the winter months. Their room was just as breathtaking, with a small navy settee and glass coffee table, ensuite with more navy tile accents and a large spa bath, and a view of the surrounding gardens.

Perhaps most breathtaking, for Zach at least, was the queen sized bed situated in the middle of the room, the four posts bare of any curtains.

Before he could stop himself, Zach turned to Soph.

"I can sleep on the settee, if you're more comfortable with that."

"Zach." He winced at the sudden flatness of her voice. "We're gonna share the bed. I'm not..." She stuttered for a second, and it was all he could do to not reach for her, comfort her however he could.

Taking a deep breath, she continued. "I'm not ignoring what you said this morning. I just need some time to think about it. But that doesn't change what we are to each other, and you'll always be my best friend. If that's ok with you...?"

His relief must have been written all over his face, because Sophia rushed on quickly. "Let's maybe keep the physical stuff to just when we're with everyone though? Please?"

Zach nodded, not trusting himself to speak right now. She was still his best friend. She just needed time to think. He could be patient a while longer. For her, he could do anything.

Even let her go? His subconsciousness was like a punch to the gut. But he knew that if he had to, he would.

Sophia relaxed into a warm smile. "The dinner doesn't start until four, so we have some time. Want to go book a couple's massage and make everyone jealous?"

"Say less, Sunflower." With a grin, Zach looped her arm through his and lead her back towards reception.

CHAPTER 26

The rehearsal dinner and wedding was quite frankly unremarkable. In fifty years when asked how it went, Zach doubted he would be able to recall anything about the event; not the abundance of lilies which kept making him sneeze, the incredibly monstrous display of chiffon and ruffled tulle that was the bride's dress, the decadent three course meal both nights that Sophia had correctly guessed the price of (the bride's parents were not very quiet about the expenses they had gone to for their daughter).

The only memorable part of the entire two days was Sophia, and even those moments with her felt like flashes of a dream. The soft skin of her lower back as he led her to her seat at the table, the press of her hand to his knee when she talked about him to other guests, the shape of her smile from across the room and the brief but intoxicating taste of strawberries and chocolate when he kissed her after dessert in front of the groom and his family.

Towards the end of the ceremony, Zach remembered gently rubbing her thigh over the silk of her emerald green gown, watching as Sophia subtly brushed away a tear.

"Are you ok?" He whispered softly in her ear as the bride and groom shared their first kiss as spouses.

Nodding, Soph kept her eyes on the couple as they stood for the exit procession.

"Actually, I am. I just realised — I'm happy for them."

"Really?" Zach kept his voice down. "I don't know, Olivia looks a bit strained if I'm being honest —"

Soph nudged him in the ribs, and he coughed to cover it up.

"You don't understand. I'm *happy* for them. When I remember that Eliot is my ex, I just kind of feel... nothing anymore."

Zach stared at her.

"Really?" He said again.

Soph smirked at him with a good natured roll of her eyes. "Really."

As they followed the stream of guests to the final reception, Sophia held tightly to his hand. Because he could, Zach pulled her wrist to his mouth and kissed over her pulse, thrilled when he felt it skip a beat. When she smiled shyly up at him, he pretended for a second that it was real.

"Thought for a thought?" He asked as they reached their assigned seats.

Sophia looked pensive, toying with a strand of hair that had fallen from her twisted up-do. "I'm wondering why we've been placed further towards the back of the hall than we originally were last night."

"Huh," Zach glanced around. He hadn't really noticed where they sat, too busy glaring at some of the male guests who hadn't got the memo that Soph was 'taken'. "Why would they move us?"

"Probably wedding politics," Sophia gestured with the roll of bread she had picked up, butterknife in her other hand. Other guests had wandered in or were already seated, and waiters were already bringing the entree out — pea soup with edible flower decorations slowly sinking into the viscous mixture.

Serving paused briefly as the wedding party and new spouses were announced. As the bridesmaids trailed behind in their bright yellow dresses, a few of them threw glares towards him and Soph.

"That seemed uncalled for, don't you think?" Zach slid an arm protectively around the back of Soph's chair.

Eliot and Liv walked past then, Eliot casting one nervous glance their way while Liv steadfastly walked straight ahead, chin high.

With a small sympathetic smile, Soph leant in closer to him. "I think poor Olivia and her friends just found out I'm Eliot's ex. I would be pretty mad too if I found out at my wedding."

"Ah." Poor Liv. Hopefully Zach's presence would be a small comfort that Soph was over Eliot and wished them no ill-will.

And if she really was over Eliot, then maybe she'd have an answer for him soon.

After dessert — and a scorching kiss that Zach made sure to savour — he and Sophia kept their status as wallflowers and watched as guests in varying states of sobriety took to the dance floor.

He couldn't stop staring at her. She was easily the most gorgeous person in the room, the green of her dress making her skin glow and her hair look like a halo. It didn't help that her dress had a halter neck, which tied into a long ribbon that flowed over her bare back, stopping just below her stunning ass. He couldn't even blame the other guests — girls and guys alike — for ogling.

Soph had been right; sometimes, he really was such a guy.

The music changed, and although the shift minuscule, Zach knew Soph well enough to notice the tension that filled her shoulders and bracketed her mouth.

"What is it Sunflower?" Zach scanned her over, checking for any signs of pallor or oncoming syncope.

Soph mock-scowled. "Stop trying to eyeball my vital signs, nerd. I'm fine."

Zach stuck his tongue out at her, letting go of the breath he hadn't realised he had been holding. "You just seem tense all of a sudden."

Leaning her head on his shoulder, Soph fiddled with the deep emerald tie he had on (and yes, he had made sure it matched her dress).

"This song... used to be our song." She gestured loosely to Eliot, who was now dancing with Liv in the centre of the room. "I'm not mad about it anymore, I don't think I have the energy to care. But it just feels a bit... weird."

"Sunflower," Zach pulled her closer, so her chest was flush against his own. "Your feelings, cheesy as this might be, are valid. I really get it, it would feel weird if I was in your place. And you never have to feel like you can't tell me just because it has to do with your past relationship. Ok? You're my best friend. I'm here for you no matter what you're feeling."

For the first time, Soph's expression was unreadable.

"Did I say something wrong?" Zach forced a grin. "Too much therapy talk?"

Soph didn't reply. She simply pressed a devastatingly soft kiss to his cheek, then dragged him onto the dance floor.

Sophia was dancing with Zach at her ex's wedding. Just that thought alone made her almost laugh out loud. But nothing, not even Eliot's occasional eye contact (try as she might to avoid it), could distract her from Zach right now.

She had been sneaking glances at him all weekend, his earlier confession on a loop in her head. And now, with him dressed like James Bond, scraping her cheek with his stubble and filling her senses with his cologne, she couldn't for the life of her remember why she hadn't just told him she wanted this to be real too.

And maybe it was a poor excuse, to try hint with her body rather than her words, but with Zach's arms wrapped around her and her breasts tight against his chest, Sophia decided that it was time to stop holding herself back from something she wanted so badly it had invaded her every dream. Timelines could go to hell.

Full of determination, Sophia pressed herself closer. Zach twirled her around then back against his chest, and as the music changed once again, Soph shifted so her arms were around his neck. Perfectly in reach of his soft brown hair, which she gently tugged at as they swayed.

Zach raised an eyebrow at her. "Really putting on a show for everyone, Sunflower."

Soph grinned, and lightly drew her nails over his scalp before twisting, her back now flush against him as they kept swaying.

"Sunflower," Zach groaned in her ear. "These pants are really tight, honey. You can't tease me like this."

"Can't I?" Soph whispered into his ear, deftly letting him spin her around again.

Two more songs passed, and as the room darkened and more people joined the floor, Soph got bolder. But so did Zach. Hands delved, kisses were exchanged, and soon everything faded until there was no-one else but them.

"Zach," Soph panted as a particularly fast rendition of 'You Belong With Me' played on full blast. "You know how I said we should try to not be physical while I worked out my feelings?"

"Yes?" His voice was raw with lust and hope, and it shot straight between her thighs.

"I take it back. Take me to bed."

It was all Zach had needed to hear. And as they ran laughing through the crowded hall back to their room, Soph only felt a slight twinge of guilt for not confessing fully herself.

CHAPTER 27

It had taken Zach three tries to use the key to their room, mostly because Sophia's hands had already been unbuttoning his pants. She didn't even remember taking off her dress. The only thing that currently mattered was Zach, lying on the bed beneath her and groaning deeply as he squeezed her thighs, her own body quivering with anticipation from where she hovered naked over him, straddling his broad chest.

God, he was gorgeous like this.

"Feast on me, baby. I know you've been dying to since the last time."

Zach leant forward slightly, eyes glazed, and Sophia pulled herself back with a laugh. His head flopped back with a groan and he squeezed her thighs again. Wiggling teasingly, Sophia dipped closer again.

"Go on," Sophia grinned wickedly, lightly dragging her nails over his stomach, up to his chest before flicking a nipple to elicit another small gasp. "Take what I'm offering before I change my mind."

His chocolate brown eyes devoured her for a second, making sure she meant what she said. Before she could punish him for hesitating, though, he started devouring *her*.

"Oh!" Sophia gasped, head lolling back as Zach's tongue lapped at the wetness spread across her inner thighs.

He felt incredible. Warm and wet and *god yes*, right there. Closer to her clit with each lick, Sophia had to breathe deeply, pace herself before letting go of her inhibitions and wantonly riding his face like she had dreamt of.

Without stopping his small licks and nibbles, Zach somehow gripped her ass and dragged her further up his chest, until she was gripping the headboard and he was finally sucking her sensitive nub until she writhed.

Her slick was dripping down her thighs, and Zach alternated between plunging strokes of his tongue and teasing laps at her folds, his beard gently scraping against her skin.

Sophia was ready to burst into flames. Pleasure zinged up her spine and pooled in her stomach, heat staining her cheeks as she unabashedly undulated her hips.

"Tell me," she whimpered, "Tell me if it's too much."

She ground down harder, chasing the release that she could feel barreling towards her.

Zach lifted her off his face for a heartbeat, pinching her clit hard enough that she saw stars.

"I could never get enough of you, Sunflower," he rasped, before diving straight between her legs again.

"I'm so close, Z," Sophia was gripping the headboard so hard her knuckles were white, and she must be suffocating Zach with how hard her thighs were squeezing his ears. But she couldn't stop, could barely see. Could only feel the constant sensation of his tongue inside her, of his large hand sneaking around the globe of her ass to the delicate skin between both cheeks —

"Fuck!"

Her orgasm crested like a wave, obliterating all conscious thought from her body. Zach didn't let up, a finger gently stroking her behind while he nibbled lightly on her clit, drawing out her pleasure until she was wrung out and holding on the bed head for dear life.

Slowly, Zach lowered her onto his chest, her legs limp on either side of his hips. His thick cock was stiff and velvety, prodding at her entrance, but he knew better than to take her without her permission.

"Are you going to make me beg, Sunflower?" Zach pressed a kiss to the top of her ear.

"I should," Soph hummed. "But you've been so good for me today."

The flush on his cheeks stoked her desire for him again. He was too good, this man. Too right for her. She relished being in control with him, dictating their pleasure like a master puppeteer. But what if she was leading them both off the edge of a cliff? Especially after his confession yesterday morning...

As if sensing the turn of her thoughts, Zach flipped her onto her side, propping one of her legs over his arm and sliding deep into her centre.

"Stop thinking," he whispered with a slow thrust. "Let me take care of you."

"I don't need to be taken care of," Sophia moaned as Zach hit an especially sensitive spot, her eyes fluttering closed.

"*I* need to take care of you, Sunflower. I need you to use me to take care of you."

Sophia opened her eyes, meeting Zach's earnest gaze. Holding her like this, open and vulnerable and still messy from his earlier ministrations, what they were doing almost felt too intimate. Too close to being something real.

"Use me, baby. Please." Soph knew that Zach was holding himself back, was going slow until she gave him an answer.

And how could she ever refuse this wonderful, attentive, caring man?

"Ok," she agreed, relaxing into his rhythm. "Now make me forget my own name."

Zach unleashed himself, a force of nature with every facet of his being focused on her, on her pleasure. Sophia didn't think she could ever get used to it, never wanted to try. With each press into her, she slid a little higher on the mattress, a little deeper in love.

Before Sophia could panic over that thought, Zach drew her leg over his shoulder, sliding even deeper somehow. Letting out a small scream, Soph dug her nails into the muscles of his shoulder, raking them over his back, his sides.

"Yes!" Zach lapped at the spot on her neck she loved. "Mark me, Sunflower. Show everyone I'm yours."

Spurred on, Sophia dragged a hand further down, tracing the black lines of ink decorating his hip. She wanted to suck at each rose petal, leave bite marks over his ass.

Speaking of his ass…

Zach was lost in her, biting and sucking at her collarbone, the tops of her breasts. Without giving a warning, she quickly slipped a small finger past the tight ring of muscle and pressed hard.

Zach came with a string of expletives, bucking into her hard enough for her to see stars. Garbled moans and sweet nothings fell from Zach's mouth as her own orgasm crashed into her again, lightening filling her veins and setting her blood on fire.

Before she could move, Zach was rocking into her again, slow and steady. Soph could feel their combined wetness between her thighs, the hard swell of Zach's cock brushing that sensitive spot inside her. He hadn't even softened.

"Don't you dare stop, Sunflower," Zach sucked her bottom lip into his mouth, nipping it lightly.

"You like that little trick?" Some fire had returned to her voice, mixed with smugness.

"God yes," Zach let out a low moan as she pressed her finger deeper once again. God, if he liked this, what else could she do to him? What else could they explore together?

Moving faster now, Zach finally released her leg and pulled away.

"If I asked you to use me, what would you say?"

This man. No one had ever been so vulnerable for her, let her be so vulnerable in return.

"I'll do anything you want me to, Z."

Zach cocked a brow at her, as though asking her to prove it.

So sitting up on her knees, Soph motioned for him to turn around. It was his turn again to be on his back.

CHAPTER 28

Zach had never felt anything like this before. Hadn't realised it was something he had craved. Oh, he knew he was kinky and that he loved his women in charge, but Soph was taking it to a whole new level.

She was on her knees for him again while he lay against the plush pillows, choking on his cock like she was starved for it. With every lick and suck, she twisted her hands expertly around his hard length, squeezing as she reached the base and making him gasp. This woman was pure magic, coaxing his pleasure like she was the only person who could give it to him.

And then Soph moved lower.

"Jesus fucking Christ!" Zach saw god for a second. Everything tingled, from his balls to his spine. Sophia was moaning as she licked at his entrance, hands not changing from their unrelenting pace as she tugged at his cock. Warmth surged from somewhere behind his navel, and Zach swore again.

"Sunflower, I need you. I need to taste you. Please." He didn't even care that he was begging.

Soph paused briefly, replacing her tongue with a finger and drawing a cry from Zach's throat. "I'm busy, Z. You can taste me later."

"Now. God, please Soph, now, now." Zach bucked his hips as she hit his prostate for the second time that night, lights exploding behind his eyes. He was so full of need he could barely think.

"Well, since you asked so nicely."

Zach let out a noise of protest as Sophia pulled away, but was quickly cut off by her gorgeous thighs straddling his face again. Without waiting for permission, he immediately latched onto her hips with a punishing grip, lavishing her hard little clit with his tongue.

Nothing had tasted so sweet in his life.

Her juices ran down his chin, and the room filled with the erotic sounds of slurping and sucking as Sophia stretched out over him and took him back into her mouth. Every time Zach hit the back of her throat, he moaned, the vibrations of his voice on her greedy clit triggering Sophia to gyrate even more, an endless cycle of pleasure.

Sophia moaned again, taking Zach somehow even deeper. It was too much now, too good, all tongue and soft lips and wet hot tightness, compounded with the salty sweet taste of her.

"Soph, baby," Zach pulled back, "You're gonna make me —"

She didn't let him finish. Instead, she slammed herself down on his cock, her nose brushing his sensitive skin, and thrust two fingers into his ass at the same time. She twisted hard, then flicked her tongue over his sensitive tip.

Coming didn't quite encapsulate what Zach did. He erupted. And Soph swallowed every last drop.

Ears ringing and vision blurry, Zach managed to realise that Soph had exploded with him and was lying equally spent over his chest, still giving him a magnificent view of her dripping pussy.

There was no way in hell Zach would settle for them being just friends anymore.

***

They had stayed wrapped in each other's arms all night, only leaving the bed to use the bathroom — or to share the shower. Despite not much sleep being had, Zach had never felt so rested. He had barely even thought about the fact that he had to be back at work in a few hours.

It was currently morning and Sophia was draped over his chest, illuminated by the golden sunlight streaming in from gaps in the curtains. Zach loved her like this — lazy, half-awake, blinking away sleep. She felt most like his in the mornings.

With a yawn, Soph stretched against him like a cat as she rubbed her eyes.

"What time is it?" She yawned again, so her question sounded more like "wha ime sit?".

"Just after nine. You can keep sleeping, I'm just looking at some emails."

"Anything interesting?" Soph propped herself onto her side, her blue eyes shockingly clear in the light.

"Actually, yes. There's a medical charity ball coming up that I've been asked to speak at, it's fundraising for kids with dyslexia. It's short notice, but I think I'll say yes."

"That sounds pretty cool. I've only ever been to conferences before, never any charity events."

Glancing up at Soph, Zach had a thought. "Why don't you come with me?"

"What? No, that wasn't me trying to invite myself. Plus I'm not a doctor."

"So? And even if you were inviting yourself, I want you there. Be my plus one. It'll be fun."

She bit her lip, and Zach had to stop himself from leaning forward to bite it for her.

"There'll be free canapés," he cajoled.

Soph scowled. "Why didn't you lead with that? Just tell me where and when."

"So I'll pick you up at seven on Thursday?"

Soph rolled her eyes, but she smiled and nodded.

Grinning from his victory, Zach moved to take off his glasses (he had worn them briefly this morning while reading before Soph woke up), but Sophia's loud noise of complaint stopped him.

"You should keep them on. I like your glasses," she said shyly.

"Yeah?" He grinned widely at her.

Shifting under the fitted sheets, Soph flashed a tease of cleavage as she turned onto her back.

"Yeah. Gives you a Clark Kent kind of vibe. You should know that makes you an instant turn on to female nerds everywhere."

"So does this make you my Lois Lane?" Zach knew his voice sounded too hopeful. Now was not the time to push her for an answer. Besides, it wouldn't be much of an answer — whatever Soph felt, it wouldn't change the fact that Zach's feelings weren't going anywhere. They were only growing stronger.

"We'll see," Soph smiled as she pulled back the blankets, walking shamelessly naked to the ensuite in the corner.

"Hate it when you walk away, but god do I love the view!" Zach called out after her.

"Oh fuck off," Zach huffed a laugh as she shut the door.

Today was going to be a good day.

CHAPTER 29

It was almost ten by the time Soph was out of the shower, and the room was empty. A note on the hotel stationery had been left on her pile of clothes, in surprisingly legible handwriting for a doctor.

GETTING US BREAKFAST SUNFLOWER. BACK IN 20!

A smiley face was crudely doodled at the bottom, and she couldn't help but smile. This weekend had turned out to be better than her wildest dreams. Stretching out over the bed in her bathrobe, hair wet from her shower, Soph enjoyed the slight twinges of pain leftover from the night before. It had been a while since she had been in certain positions for that long, and her yoga classes with Nef didn't count.

Everything just felt so easy with Zach. And very far from the realm of pretend. After this morning, there didn't seem to be any reason to not give in anymore. They wanted each other, plain and simple. And clearly they worked, as friends and on a more physical level. Sure, it might be a little sooner than most people would expect, but screw that. She was twenty nine, a full fledged adult with a job and a life that was hers to control. And after everything, she knew best how important it was to grab the good things in life with both hands when the opportunity arose.

A knock on the door interrupted her thoughts.

"It's open, Z!" She called out. Trust Zach to forget his key card.

The clearing of a throat made her sit up like a rocket, her head spinning slightly at her speed.

"Eliot?" She could barely choke his name out. "What are you doing?"

The 'here' was implied. Drawing her bathrobe tighter around her, Soph shuffled to the end of the bed so she was standing as well.

Eliot looked… rough, if she was being honest. Sandy hair uncharacteristically unstyled, hotel one size fits all slippers on his feet, and she was pretty sure his shirt was the same one from the reception the night before.

"Eliot?" She prompted the silence again.

He stepped forward, hands in his pockets and barely meeting her gaze. "Hey, Soph. Can we talk?"

"Considering you're in my hotel room, at your wedding, do I have a choice?" She said acerbically.

"I wanted to apologise. I know I screwed up." He met her eyes then, and he looked to be genuinely upset.

But fuck, that wasn't her problem.

"Apologising after you've married another woman is firstly, not the right time. Second, I actually ran out of fucks to give months ago, so please feel free to leave and go back to your wife and leave me — and my boyfriend," she added quickly, the word weirdly comfortable in her mouth, "alone."

"You don't understand," he sounded like a petulant teenager. "I love Liv. And I know I should have ended it with you way before starting anything with her —"

"You think?" Soph snapped.

"— but my parents let it slip that you're my ex and now she realised that she was the other woman. She's really pissed at me." Eliot wrung his hands together. He looked so lost, she almost felt sorry for him.

"Your marriage, your problem. Why did you come to me?" Soph knew she was being pretty harsh. But actually hearing Eliot confirm that he just married the woman he had cheated on her with wasn't really making her feel all warm and fuzzy, surprisingly.

Eliot ran a hand through his hair, making it stick up even more, greasy from all the gel he hadn't yet washed out. "I was hoping… well I was hoping that maybe you'd talk to Liv. Tell her that it's all behind us and that there's no bad blood anymore."

Soph's heart stopped, before it resumed its pounding against her chest. Red washed over her vision, before settling into a pool of ice that spread through her veins.

"Eliot," she smiled sweetly and stepped closer, almost toe to toe with him. Looking up into his eyes, she softened for a moment, their shared history crashing over her. "You cheated on me. You dumped me publicly. You married the other woman. You proposed to her with the ring you had meant to buy me."

Eliot blanched, hands raised as though to defend himself against her verbal onslaught, but Soph didn't stop. Pulling herself up to her full height, she drew in a deep breath and released the weight that had been sitting on her chest for months.

"I want you to know: I forgive you. Because I can't be fucked to waste time holding a grudge on someone who doesn't mean anything to me. But you can be damned to hell and back if you think I will ever do you a single favour, let alone talk to your wife for you about your mistakes and lies. I hope for your sake that you can grow up and be the husband she deserves. Now get out of my room."

Eliot looked ready to flee for his life. But as he reached the doorway, he stopped and looked back.

"I really am sorry, Soph. I know it doesn't mean much now, but I still love you. You'll always be important to me. Just think about what I asked."

Before she could throw her own slipper at him for his sheer audacity, he left, closing the door behind him.

Slumping back on the bed, Soph tugged at her hair with a groan when another knock sounded at the door.

"What!" She shouted.

"Damn, Sunflower," Zach strode in with a heavy tray, loaded with various fruits, pastries, and what looked like half the bacon in the building. "Good thing I got us breakfast cause you seem pretty hangry."

Soph let out an angry huff, ready to tell him everything that had happened. But when she looked up, Zach's face looked stormy.

"What's wrong?" She furrowed her brows.

"I saw Eliot leaving."

Soph rolled her eyes. "Good riddance to him. You won't believe what he asked me to do."

"Are you sure it's good riddance?" Zach's face was like stone.

"What do you mean?"

"He looked pretty cosy in his slippers and shirt from last night."

"If you're trying to imply something, spit it out. If you can't remember, I was with you all last night."

"You're right. I'm sorry Sunflower. I just saw him and heard him say he loves you, and I just…" Zach grabbed at his hair, rumpling the loose curls. It looked way hotter rumpled like this on him than it had on Eliot.

Deflating, Soph nodded her understanding. If the scenario was flipped, if she had seen his ex leaving his room early in the morning looking rumpled, her mind would have also gone straight to worst case scenario.

"I'm sorry," Zach repeated, drawing her into a hug.

Soph melted into his arms. Nothing made her as comfortable as having her head against Zach's chest. It was like he had been made for her, every divot and muscle designed to fit with her own.

Pressing her nose to his collar, Soph mumbled quietly. "Half of why I fell for you was because of how amazing you've been with me throughout this whole shitty situation."

Zach stiffened, but said nothing.

"I'm not really hungry at the moment. I think I'm going to take a walk? I just need to cool down. Eliot shoved way too much testosterone in my face and I need to do something before I snap and use him for phlebotomy practice."

Zach laughed. "Do whatever you need, Sunflower. I'll be here when you get back."

Giving him one last squeeze, Soph ditched the bathrobe and got dressed, glad she had thought to pack her favourite jeans. Before she left, she tossed a quick goodbye over her shoulder.

"I'll be back in about an hour! Love you!"

It was only when she reached the garden that she realised what she had said.

CHAPTER 30

Soph had always loved the dentist. She loved the way her dentist would explain what he was doing as he was doing it, the taste of the bubblegum foam they always used at the end to help whiten her teeth. If she hadn't gone into medical research, maybe she would have tried to be a dentist. But what she had loved most of all was the huge fish tank they had in the waiting room.

Even today, Soph would go to the same dentist twice a year. She'd show up half an hour early, and would take a seat opposite the tank where she'd mindlessly watch the myriad of angel fish and guppies and bottom feeders swim through the bubbles and sea grass. It always calmed her. So it was no surprise that she found herself forty five minutes later sitting on a bench in the back garden, watching a bunch of koi swim in one of the only filled fountains.

She loved Zach. Was in love with him. And had finally vented at her ex. Instead of the jubilance she had expected to feel, she just felt... content. Not elated, not triumphant, not vengeful. Just... normal. Like she had been sailing through the Drake Passage and had finally docked on solid land.

Sighing, Soph moved closer to the fountain and dipped a finger into the freezing water, smiling slightly as a curious koi came to nibble on the potential snack.

"Not for you, fishy," she murmured.

The sound of her name being called made her look up sharply, then silently groan.

Liv was crossing the garden, heading straight for her. Soph had no ill will towards her, but man was she the last person she needed to see right now.

"Liv, I'm so sorry but I'm not in the mood to talk right now," Soph started to say as she got closer.

"Sophia, Eliot just told me that he saw you and what he asked of you, and I just wanted to come and say that I am so sorry."

"What?" Soph blinked up at the woman.

"I'm so sorry." Liv repeated, sitting down on the ledge next to Soph. "For Eliot's audacity to ask anything of you, and for, well, him and me. I promise you, I had no idea he was in a relationship with anyone while we were dating. I didn't even think he had an ex!"

Her voice had risen, half panicked and half devastated.

"I just wanted to tell you myself that I never would have even considered dating him if I had known, and that I'm disgusted with him and with myself for marrying someone who'd do that."

Soph still didn't know what to say. This had not been what she'd been expecting from Liv.

"Anyway, I, I know this is a shock, and honestly I'm so impressed you even came to the wedding at all. And I know we haven't known each other long, but I think you're wonderful, and I hope Zach treats you better than Eliot could ever dream. I just wanted you to hear from me first, but I'm going to annul the wedding tonight."

"What?" God, she had been turned into a broken record.

"I was the other woman. Aside from feeling awful about how you were treated, I'm disgusted that Eliot thinks I'd find out and reward his behaviour by still marrying him. That's not who I want to be." Liv sniffled and shrugged, and the two lapsed into a thoughtful silence.

Minutes ticked past, and Liv must have become uncomfortable because she stood to leave.

"Wait." Soph grabbed her hand. "Don't go yet."

It was Liv's turn to look shocked.

"Eliot... he isn't a bad guy." Soph cringed. "I mean, he's done some bad things, obviously, but he clearly does love you. Enough to propose after god knows how long when he wouldn't propose to me after five years."

Both women shared a watery laugh.

"What he did to me... to us, it isn't your fault. I won't tell you what to do cause it's your relationship — and I think you're equally brave for even thinking about an annulment after you just had this whole grand event. But this is your relationship now. I don't want to be a part of it, or a factor that influences it. What's happened has happened, and I'm happy now." With a shock, Soph realised it was true. She was happy now. Zach made her happy.

"Eliot didn't put you up to this?" Liv was sniffling harder now.

Soph made a face of disgust. "Liv, I like you. Do you really think I'd do anything for Eliot at this point in time?"

They laughed again, smiling through tears. At some point, the two of them had clasped hands.

"You deserve to be happy Liv, really. And I don't think it'll hurt to force Eliot to face the consequences of his actions."

"That's what my Dad told me," Liv chuckled. "I do — did, whatever — really love him. But there's so much going through my head now."

Soph stayed quiet, letting Liv rant.

"Like how on earth could I even start a marriage based on lies? What kind of person did I marry if he didn't even bother to tell me you were his ex? Or that he invited his ex to the wedding? It's like, the biggest betrayal of trust. It's a deal breaker for me. The person I thought I knew, he doesn't exist. And then his audacity to ask you to clean up his mess? He's like a child. I'd end up having to mother the man who's supposed to be an adult already. " Liv was almost yelling now, face flushed with pent up anger. "No offence to you, of course, it was lovely meeting you."

Soph couldn't help but giggle. "He really is kind of a dick, isn't he?"

The two women started sniggering. Then cackling. Tears rolled down Soph's cheeks, and by the time they both settled she could definitely feel herself wheezing a bit.

"So," Sophia said more seriously. "Will you really go through with the annulment?"

Liv looked at her hands, clasped tightly in her lap, and nodded. "Him cheating on you with me isn't my responsibility. But his actions towards me while doing that, and after, have shown me that he's not the man I thought I knew, and definitely not the man I deserve. I deserve someone who puts me first and has enough respect to not make me a dirty secret until it's convenient. I deserve someone who doesn't treat his ex's like shit because of his own underlying insecurities."

"You're a good person, Liv." Soph leant her head on her new friend's shoulder. "If you ever feel really angry, give me names and I'll sign them up for clinical trials that involve lots of injections. We can start with Eliot."

Liv snorted. "I'll take you up on that."

They stared at the fish together, sharing the quiet company of two people who were emotionally exhausted but finally at peace.

"Oh, before I go," Liv stood up and held out her hand. "I think this really belongs to you."

Soph gaped. In Liv's palm was her engagement ring - the one meant for Sophia.

"Liv, I couldn't."

"Oh you so can. God knows I'm never wearing it again. Sell it, chuck it, keep it as a memento. Or just wear it as an every day ring so you can laugh every time you look at it. But it never really belonged to me. It would make me smile knowing you have it."

Reluctantly, Soph plucked the ring out of Liv's hand and slid it onto the middle finger of her right hand.

"See?" Liv smiled. "The perfect reminder. When Zach proposes, I'm sure you'll have an even better one."

With that, Liv strode back into the hotel, long coat flapping behind her in the wind.

Sophia sighed, alone again by the fountain. What a morning. She stared at her new ring, flashing in the weak winter sunlight. It really was better as an every day ring. Thank god she had never married Eliot. She smiled, thinking back to their breakup. Sure it had sucked, but if it hadn't been for that night, she never would have officially met Zach.

Thoughts drifting back to her best friend, she absentmindedly rubbed at her chest. Who would have thought the man who started as her boss would have ended up becoming the most important person in her life? Even with their earlier scuffle, Soph knew there was no one she'd rather argue and make up with.

No one she had ever loved like this before.

Standing suddenly enough to frighten the fish, Soph broke into a run back to their hotel room.

She loved Zach. And he deserved a better confession than the one she had thrown over her shoulder earlier.

CHAPTER 31

Zach really hoped that the note he had left would stop Sophia from castrating him for ditching her. Well, the note, the bouquet of red roses he had sent to her apartment for when she got home, and the pair of Jimmy Choo heels she had looked ready to cut off a guest's feet for at the wedding.

In his defence, he really hadn't had a choice. One of the patients in the trial had had an anaphylactic reaction to the increased dose they had given that morning, and one of his general patients' MRI results came back looking like a Christmas tree. With too many doctors on leave still, there was no way he could ignore his pager any longer, despite his promise to wait for Soph to get back from her walk.

Hopefully, Sophia would only kill him with words, not actions. Though death by her hand would be a pretty good death.

Unfortunately, the week blew past without them running into each other. Finn claimed to have seen her for lunch, but the only communication Zach got was a few back and forth texts whenever he got a quick break, plus a very detailed voice mail explaining her conversation with Liv. He had responded with a series of gifs emphasising his shock, and Soph had hearted each one.

Even digitally, Soph's presence soothed him. It helped that they had smoothed over their argument, with Zach apologising again profusely and Sophia telling him that next time he didn't need to buy her shoes (although she wouldn't say no considering he was the one on an attending's salary). The rest of their texts had been mutual digs at Angelo, who seemed to have become extra stuffy after the Christmas period, and praise for Bridget, who had just received her own grant for another research project.

The afternoon before the charity event, Zach was pacing in his living room while mentally reciting his speech. It was still early before he had to pick up Sophia, but he liked the extra practice. Scripts were useless for him, and while it would be great to show dyslexic kids that it was ok to use a hundred or so cue cards with size fifty font, he wanted to also show them that it was ok to find other ways to complete tasks instead. In his case, Zach would dictate to an app that would transcribe his speech, and then read it back to him at the click of a button. This way, he could memorise it faster and without worrying about stumbling over words. It was how he prepared for all his conferences, but sadly was a bit too informal when it came to writing reports.

A vibration in his pocket pulled him into stillness. It was Soph.

Z I'M SO SORRY I'M RUNNING LATE! LAST MINUTE MANDATORY MEETING WITH BRIDGET. WILL UBER OVER AND SHOULD MAKE IT IN TIME FOR YOUR SPEECH. SORRY AGAIN!!

Damn. Fair enough though, when Bridget called you didn't really say no. But he had so been looking forward to picking her up, walking in to the event together. And now that the wedding was over, they needed to talk about the whole fake dating situation.

Maybe he should call Mira to pass the time while he waited. He needed to do something, at least. The waiting was always the worst, and Zach always went into admin mode, not able to do anything but focus on the upcoming commitment. Itching to move, Zach resumed his pacing while speed dialling Mira.

"I hope you're calling to tell me how this fake dating crap went," Mira's voice was sugary sweet.

"Why do you sound like you know something I don't?"

"Because I always know something you don't, brother dear."

Zach sighed. "The fake dating was fine. How are you going?"

"Oh no, Zach, you don't get to change the subject just yet. Elaborate on 'fine'."

Zach rolled his eyes at her insistence.

"And don't roll your eyes at me."

"Jesus, Ra-Ra, are you stalking me?"

"I wish, Z. Then I'd know about how you and Sophia are going without having to wait for you to call."

He sighed again, his new signature response when talking to his sister.

"Fine. It went basically how you expected, and I can guarantee you don't want to know any more details. She's coming with me tonight to that charity ball I was telling you about earlier."

"Where you'll confess your lurveeee?"

"This is why I don't talk to you about my dating life."

Mira cackled loudly. "You love her, you love her!" She sang.

"Ok I'm hanging up now." Zach put his phone back in his pocket, scowling. This was not what he needed right before a big speech — both for the charity ball and for the woman he'd fallen in love with.

His phone buzzed violently, and he picked up with another long-suffering sigh.

"All I meant to say, Z," Mira said gently, "is that I'm happy for you. And I really hope it works out."

"Thanks, Mira."

***

The ballroom was packed. Danilo was running a tight ship as usual, aided this year by Xander and his fiancée, who had opened up their museum for the night for this private event. The place looked spectacular: instead of the previous exhibition that Soph had described to him, with columns and olive trees and fairy lights, Sophia's best friend had created the illusion of a jungle paradise.

Potted palm trees lit from below towered towards the arched roof, and vines dripped from the edges of the crown moulding. Various artefacts were framed against portable walls, strategically placed to create a maze like pattern leading to the raised platform at the back of the hall. Instead of music, the sound of laughter and guests chattering mixed with bird sounds and rainfall, projecting from hidden speakers. And speaking of rain, the light fixtures were like something out of a movie; there was no large light, only minuscule droplets of warm yellow spots, encased in individual glass tear drops and dangling at various heights from the ceiling. It looked like it was raining, a downfall set on fire and paused just before it hit the guests.

Slightly less covered in the jungle theme, a table by the large front doors was decorated with raffles, manned by staff in charge of confirming each guest's place on the invite list. It was here that Zach waited with Danilo before giving his speech, where he had a clear line of site for every entering guest, trying not to get too excited with every blonde woman he saw.

But fifteen minutes turned into half an hour, and Sophia still hadn't arrived. He hadn't gotten any more texts from her, either. He debated heading outside to see if he could call her, but Danilo caught his arm at the exit.

"Speech time, Doc," the handsome middle aged Brazilian winked at him.

With one last longing look towards the doors, Zach made his way to the podium. He didn't even care if Soph missed his speech. He just wanted her to show up.

CHAPTER 32

Sophia realised that she just had to accept it: Zach was magnetic to watch no matter the context. But here, standing under the ephemeral raindrops of light with Nef, watching him gesture to the crowd like he was at a Ted Talk, everything seemed amplified.

Thank god she had made it in time, had packed her outfit to work again. Bridget had taken one look at her in her office, in the sparkly shoes Zach had bought her and a matching silver dress (a longer, more formal version of the dress she had first met Zach in) and had immediately rescheduled the meeting.

"No dress with that kind of neckline takes a backseat to a research update," Bridget had said. "Even doctors need to remember to have a life sometimes."

Soph smiled at the memory, then at the way Zach was currently moving across the stage, the crowd hanging on to his every word.

"So," Nef sipped at a glass of champagne, her dark hair cascading down the back of her long sleeved black gown. "How's your health?"

Without looking away from Zach's closing words, Soph furrowed her brows. "Fine? Why?"

"Oh, you know. You've just been spending a lot of time with a doctor, last I've heard."

Of course Nef knew. A twinge of guilt went through her for not telling her best friend sooner. But between the night of the wedding, Eliot's antics, and then Zach having to deal with medical emergencies leaving the bulk of final data analysis to her, Soph had felt too overwhelmed. If she was being honest, she still hadn't quite processed everything — or what she was planning to do tonight.

"I'll tell you everything, Nef, I promise. I'm still, I just…" Soph trailed off, smoothing a hand over her brow. This hairstyle was way too tight, that must be why she felt a headache coming on.

"Oh honey," Nef pulled her into a tight hug as the room broke out into applause for Zach's speech. "I don't care what you tell me — though you owe me details for all the details I gave you about me and Xander. I just want you to be happy."

"I know," Soph mumbled, squished against her much taller friend's chest. Pulling away, she checked that her makeup was still in place

"He makes me happy," she admitted softly. "I think I've just been so caught up in the idea of timelines that I didn't want to do anything too soon."

Nef nodded in understanding. "You've always worried what other people thought of your relationship with Eliot. Of course you wouldn't want people to think you're rushing in to this now."

"It's not just that," Soph protested. "With Eliot, I worried about what others thought because there would be moments here or there where he'd make some off comment, and I would be embarrassed, or concerned about how others might interpret it."

Soph paused, thinking back to multiple dinner parties that she typically only replayed at three in the morning when she was too embarrassed to sleep.

"With Zach," she continued, "I'm scared that I'm doing the same thing Eliot did to me by moving on too soon."

Nef turned and took Soph by the shoulders, ignoring the annoyed huff of someone behind them who now couldn't see the stage.

"Sophia May Adkins." Oh shit, Nef had brought out the big guns. "Eliot cheating on you is a universe away from you moving on with a wonderful man who treats you right when you've been single for months."

Hanging her head, Soph nodded reluctantly. Just because her head knew it was true didn't mean her heart cooperated.

"Actually, I need to update you about Eliot and Liv."

"We like Liv, right?" Nef sipped from her champagne.

"Yeah, we do." Zach had stepped back from the podium now, and a smartly dressed black man with an Egyptian accent was now speaking. "Liv's annulling the wedding."

Nef choked, earning her another glare from a guest. She glared right back, and the man sidled away quickly.

"What happened?" Nef was incredulous.

Soph smiled. "She was kind of amazing, actually. She found out she had been the other woman, apologised to me, and told me how she deserves better than being a second chance or a secret fling until Eliot wanted more."

Nef nodded her approval. "Good for her. No one deserves to start a relationship that way. Plus, how can she be sure he won't just do the same to her?"

"Exactly! That's what she said too."

"We should take her for brunch."

Soph snorted. "As much as I like her, I don't think I'd want to get brunch with my ex's ex if I was in her shoes. Let's leave her to put this all behind her."

Sneaking a canapé off a passing tray, Nef mumbled around a mouthful. "While we wait for these speeches to end, want to tell me about all the times Zach's been behind you?"

It was Sophia's turn to choke.

"Christ, Nef. Not here!"

"Come on, just give me a number. Eight? Ten?"

Nudging her friend in the ribs, Soph shook with silent laughter. "Just cause your book boyfriends have massive dicks doesn't mean men in real life do. And don't tell me anything else about Xander or I swear to god."

Neg waggled her eyebrows. Sighing, Soph subtly pulled her hands apart, watching as Nef's mouth dropped open first with shock, then silent appreciation.

"Nice," she smirked.

"Been there, done that." Soph smirked back.

Just then, Xander appeared behind Nef, placing a quick kiss to the side of his fiancée's neck.

"Hey Sophia," Xander grinned. He pressed a kiss to Nef's temple. "How're you going? Don't usually see you at these events."

"I'm here with Zach." Soph gestured towards the podium.

"Dr Hayes?" Xander quirked an eyebrow. "We've met briefly before but never had a chance to properly talk. He gave a good speech."

"He's a great speaker. A great doctor, too." Soph said proudly.

"Great in the sack as well, apparently," Nef muttered wickedly.

Stepping not so subtly on Nef's toe, Soph redirected the conversation before Xander caught on.

"How's work, Xander?"

The tall auburn haired man shrugged. "Same as usual. We're thinking of expanding the museum later this year, actually. We need more space and want to be able to host multiple events like these at once."

"That's amazing!" Soph had never been prouder of her friends. "Tiye will be so excited."

Nef smiled at the mention of her aunt, who was the museum's previous custodian.

"Hey, Asim's finished his speech." Xander raised a hand towards the black man on the podium, who flashed a blinding grin and started heading towards them. "Soph, can you introduce me to Zach properly please?"

Nef elbowed him gently. "Soph needs some time alone with him first."

Xander frowned. "I feel like I'm missing something here."

Nef turned to fill him in, and Soph laughed as she made her short goodbyes. It was about time she finally talked to Zach.

CHAPTER 33

With each step Soph took closer to Zach, she could feel her palms growing sweaty and her heart jump in her chest. She hadn't felt this nervous in years. It was stupid — she knew how he felt. But what if she had taken too much time to tell him she felt the same? What if he had realised she wasn't worth the effort?

But then she looked at him, standing tall in the crowd, and it was like magic. Something made him look up at the same time, and as their eyes met, Zach broke into a smile so wide it could have lit up the entire museum.

It was a miracle they didn't bowl each other over, they practically ran to each other.

"I feel like I haven't seen you in forever!" Zach twirled her around, lowering her back to the floor slowly so that her breasts dragged over his chest. "I'm so glad you came."

"You're an incredible public speaker. When our paper gets us invited to conferences, I'm making you do the talking." Soph hadn't stepped back, hadn't moved her arms from their rightful place around Zach's neck.

It didn't matter that everyone was sneaking (not so subtle) glances at them, or that a handsome looking Brazilian couple had clearly edged closer to try eavesdrop. The only thing that mattered was the man standing in front of her. Her best friend. The man she loved.

"Zach, I need to tell you something."

"About that night…"

She and Zach spoke at the same time, then laughed softly.

"You first," Soph gestured, stepping back and wringing her hands. Zach ran a hand through his hair. Did he look… nervous?

"I just wanted to say I don't want to push you. And I want you to take all the time you need, whether you decide you want to make things between us real or not. I'm a patient man, and you're more than worth the wait. But if you decide you want to just stay friends, then that's more than enough for me. I'm just grateful to have you in my life." His voice cracked slightly, and he coughed.

"Z…" Words would never be enough for what Soph felt for him. So she did the next best thing. And kissed him.

For a moment, Zach didn't move, and Soph panicked that she had somehow read things wrong. But then a switch flipped, and all of a sudden she was being pulled closer than she had thought possible. His hands were everywhere — on her back, her hips, the curve of her waist, and he wasn't kissing her so much as devouring her. She barely had time to pause for a breath before Zach's mouth was on hers again, his hands moving up her body to frame her face before sliding to her nape, holding her in place until she had been so deeply plundered she felt boneless.

Pulling back, Zach pressed their foreheads together, ignoring the mixture of whoops and mutters of "get a room".

"I know that seemed pretty self-explanatory, but just so I know I'm not misreading anything, care to spell it out for me Sunflower?" Zach's eyes sparkled.

Pressing one more kiss to his mouth, Soph took a deep breath, drawing herself back to earth.

"What I was going to say," she started, "is that there hasn't been anything fake about what I feel for you for a very long time. And I wish I had acted on it sooner, because you're not just a good doctor, you're a good man. *My* man, if you'll have me."

A cocky grin spread across Zach's face. "Can I have you riding my face again?"

"Zach!" Soph squawked. But he was already kissing her again, slow and sweet and perfect.

***

It seemed they had a habit of leaving important events early. Fortunately, neither of them had driven themselves, so one scandalised Uber driver later, they were back at Zach's, making out like teenaged virgins.

Pushing through Zach's bedroom door, Sophia forgot her own name when he licked deep into her mouth before biting her bottom lip. Moaning, she fisted her hands in his hair and moved her attention to his neck, relishing the burn of his stubble over her cheek. Sucking at the point where his neck met his shoulder, Sophia kissed his fluttering pulse before biting his collarbone hard, kissing softly over the mark in apology.

The world suddenly flipped around her. Eyes opening in surprise, she realised she was now pressed against the back of the door, legs wrapped around Zach's waist, his hands kneading her ass.

He growled low in her ear, hips grinding gently at that sensitive spot between her thighs.

"Tell me this means we're officially dating," Zach demanded, lips travelling to the tops of her breasts. Her dress was slipping down slowly, and she needed it off.

"Yes!" Soph gasped as Zach lowered her back to the floor, tugging the straps of the gown down her arms.

He made a satisfied noise, then flipped her again so her front was pressed against this door.

Wow. She was really loving this door.

And this man.

Finding the concealed zipper at her side, Zach yanked it down until the dress pooled at her feet.

"Leave the heels on," he rasped.

Soph raised an eyebrow.

"Please," he added with a lopsided flash of teeth.

Zach fell to his knees. "So good to me, Sunflower. No panties or bra. This a reward for me?"

Soph could only nod as he leant forward and dragged his tongue through her folds. Stars burst in front of her eyes when he gently tugged at her clit with his teeth, before sucking it into his mouth and swirling his tongue like he was eating an ice cream.

"So good," Zach moaned against her pussy. "My girlfriend is so sweet for me."

Her head dropped back against the door, knees trembling.

"Zach," she panted. "I —"

"I know, Sunflower. I've got you."

He did have her, body and soul. And as he braced an arm across her hips to hold her up, his other hand adding two, then three fingers in a delicious pumping rhythm that matched each stroke of his tongue, Sophia fell apart.

Shaking in the aftermath of her orgasm, she couldn't speak as Zach didn't even let up. He was licking her like a starving man, pressing hot open mouthed kisses to her inner thigh.

Lashes fluttering, Soph pushed Zach away belatedly. "No more. Too sensitive."

Zach chuckled darkly, and hell if the sound didn't travel down every nerve ending, causing her to clench her thighs tight.

"Too sensitive in general, or just for me to keep eating my favourite meal?"

Soph bit her lip, groaning. How did she not already know that Zach talked so dirty in bed? That was her job.

Grinning slyly, Soph stepped around a still-kneeling Zach towards the bed. Lying down, she spread her legs wide, arched her back and tugged on her nipples, pleased when she saw Zach's face war between adoration and savage hunger.

"Come on, boyfriend. You've been so patient waiting for me."

She watched as Zach mouthed 'boyfriend' silently to himself in wonder, her own chest tight with emotion. Catching her watching him, he shot her a quick crooked grin, wiping away remnants of her arousal from his chin with a hand. Prowling towards her, he slowly unbuckled his belt and loosened his tie, shedding clothing behind him until he was holding himself above her on the bed.

"Does this mean I can take care of you?" Zach whispered against her lips.

Pulling him closer, Sophia ran her hands over the muscles in his arms, his upper back, lower. The head of his cock brushed her opening, his pre cum mixing with the wetness still glistening between her thighs.

"We take care of each other." Soph punctuated each word with a kiss, over his brow, his nose, his chin. Finally, his mouth, groaning into the warm minty taste of him.

The feel of Zach sliding inside her was life changing. Soph was certain it would always feel this way — like coming home.

EPILOGUE

One year later

The cake was a precarious mountain of blue buttercream, and it sat in the middle of the wooden table flanked by plates of canapés and drinks. Everywhere Zach looked, people were dancing or yelling at each other over the music, Bridget long ago having dominated the playlist with the latest K-Pop band.

Everything had gone perfectly according to plan.

Last week: the Lancet officially published Zach and Sophia's research paper; they were officially Adkins and Hayes et al, 2024. Three days ago, he had planned a surprise celebration party for Soph, hosted at their new home which they had bought last month. This morning, he had written in white icing over the cake's surface "Congratulations Future Dr Sophia Adkins, PhD". And now, as his girlfriend boogied on down in the living room with Nef, Lilah, and Zara, he drew a hand to the back pocket of his jeans, checking that the other surprise he had in store hadn't magically disappeared.

This last year had been beyond Zach's wildest dreams. After completing their research, Soph had gotten a temporary research position in Sydney, Australia for a semester. It had been a long five months of figuring out time differences and falling asleep on FaceTime, but had been eased by a week-long trip to visit, where Zach was more than happy to show her sights from his childhood. It was then that he had begged her to move in with him — and after a few more months of begging, she had finally said yes.

Every day had only solidified what Zach already knew — this was it for him. And with every charity event Soph had attended with him, every family dinner she brought him home for, and the dead giveaway of a serious conversation several months back, he knew she felt the same.

Trying to find the right time to pop the question was hard, though. Too soon, and it would feel rushed. Too late, and he worried that he'd hurt her the way Eliot had. A rush of nerves flooded him as he debated yet again whether today was the right day or not.

"You look almost as green as I did," Xander drawled from over his shoulder.

Zach snorted. Having known Xander briefly from various charity events in the past, the two had become fast friends — and not just because of their partners' own close relationship.

"You, nervous? I don't believe it."

Xander barked a laugh. "It's half the reason I knew Nef was worth it. No one challenged me like she did. Like she does."

Zach smiled as his friend's face softened. Nef had been a gorgeous bride, and Sophia the perfect maid of honour. How Nef had kept today a secret was beyond him, especially when she was so keen to return the favour.

Someone had wrestled the playlist back from Bridget, and was playing something from the top 100. Soph was still dancing, practically glowing in a white dress with a sweetheart neckline and loose skirt. She was wearing her favourite shoes, the ones Zach had gotten her all those months ago.

Thinking back on Xander's words as they stood silently side by side, Zach concluded that Soph did challenge him. She made him want to be a better doctor, a better man, a better partner. She challenged him to be the best version of himself, so he could always be present for her, be the man she deserved to have in her life.

And today he would promise her to be that man for the rest of their lives and beyond, if she'd let him.

The sound of the music suddenly cutting off and Sophia's melodic voice drew him from his thoughts. It was time for speeches. With an encouraging nod and squeeze of his shoulder, Xander wandered back to Nef's side as Soph called for everyone's attention.

"Thank you so much everyone for coming! I won't talk about my upcoming PhD because I know I've already bored most of you to death with it, and I won't talk about mine and Zach's publication either for similar reasons." Light laughs came from around the crowded room. "Before I do move on from these topics though, I want to pull Zach up here too, so he can also be celebrated for his hard work."

The crowd parted and people pulled Zach towards the table of food. Looking out at the crowd of friends and family, Zach grinned as he caught site of Mira, Angelo and Finn, Soph's parents. It was almost time.

"Most of you know that this is a surprise party," Soph continued. "But there's one of you who hasn't realised yet that they're not the mastermind behind this."

Zach frowned at his girlfriend. What was she talking about?

Moving closer to him, Soph gave his hand a reassuring squeeze, her smile lighting up the entire building. Then, she dropped to one knee and pulled out a small black box.

"Zach," Sophia's voice was a cacophony of love, adoration, shyness, and hope, quiet enough for just him to hear. "You've been my rock since the moment I've met you. I know this isn't traditional, and I know you'd never make me wait. But to quote your favourite movie, "when you find the person you want to spend the rest of your life with, you want the rest of your life to start as soon as possible." And I want it to be you and me for the rest of our lives, nothing fake about it. Will you marry me?"

The room was pin-drop silent as the blood rushed through Zach's ears. For some reason, his vision was a bit cloudy, like looking through water. Chest tight and overcome with emotion, Zach responded the only way he could. He dropped to his knee, and pulled out the ring box he had been carrying everywhere for the last three months.

It was perfect, if he did say so himself — it had a low setting so it would fit under her lab gloves, came with a special chain so she could wear it around her neck when she needed to be completely sterile with research participants, and was an elegant round yellow diamond surrounded by a halo of small clear diamonds. Framed by the plain white gold band, it reminded him of a sunflower.

Sophia didn't even look at it when she threw herself into his arms, nodding her head and stuttering "yes" on repeat.

And as the room cheered and the music turned back on, as Zach and Soph slid their rings onto each other's fingers, he couldn't look away from her either. From his future, glowing as brightly as the sun.

ACKNOWLEDGEMENTS

I still find it absolutely insane to have written a second book, and that this has spun into what I am planning to be a trilogy of stand alone's! I hope you enjoyed Sophia and Zach's journey, and I can't wait to share more stories with you soon.

A massive thank you and big hugs to these people for their love, support, encouragement, beta-reading, feedback, and for keeping me sane and grounded through writing and my studies:

Adam, D, Ez, Mum, Dad, Mimi, Suzie, Gali, Caitlin, Kels, Mads, Jake, Loren, Bridgie, Ailish, Jenny, Jess, Lauren, Hana, Veera, Faith, Gracie, Anila, Bar, Ella, Isabella, Tyla, Ze'ev, Alex, Sam, and all my other ARC readers and friends who cheered me on from the moment this moved from my notes app to an actual document.

I would also like to extend a huge thank you to Pop Canberra, The Book Cow, and Paperchain for holding my book on your shelves. If you lovely readers are ever in the ACT, stop by these bookshops!! And never stop supporting Indie authors and Indie bookstores.

While my first book was the result of a galaxy of love and support from the aforementioned people and more, this book is also a result of the unbelievable encouragement, support, love, and excitement from you, my cherished readers.

Everyone who read 'The Archeologist', who liked, shared, or saved a social media post, who passed my book on to friends and followers, who bought my book online or in local stores, who messaged me or commented about how much you loved it, you made this second book possible. I had never imagined such a welcoming and enthusiastic response, and I am infinitely grateful to each and everyone one of you.

LIKED THIS?

The best way to help grow an indie author's business and skill is to leave kind and comprehensive reviews! If you liked this book, want to help support my work, or have any feedback, reviews are the best thing you can do after reading it.

I would love to hear your opinion if you have the time to leave a review on Goodreads or Amazon.

Thank you again for taking a chance on my book!

ABOUT THE AUTHOR

Evelyn Astra is a pseudonym. Evelyn is an author second, and a postgraduate university student first. She lives in Australia, loves her family's dog (and her partner), and her favourite colour is red. You can often catch her reading steamy romance novels in between doing flashcards. This is the second stand-alone-style book in her *The Professionals* series.

Get in touch with Evelyn and keep up to date with the latest news about *The Professionals*!

@evelyn_astra_author on Instagram
astraevelyn1@gmail.com